VOW TO TRUST

A FLYING CROSS RANCH ROMANCE
BOOK FOUR

SHANAE JOHNSON

THOSE JOHNSON GIRLS

CHAPTER ONE

The *plop plop plop* sound of the stone skipping across the surface of the water wasn't calming. It was the number of skips that was satisfying to Toni Solis.

Six skips brushing light kisses on the water's rim. Six plops that left behind a concentric circle of ripples before a final splash. Always the same pattern each time. That's what satisfied her.

With the stone sinking into the pool of water after its performance, Toni went back to her lists. A number of columns decorated the single page in straight lines. A lineup of duty made its way down the page on the right. On the lefthand side of the page was a series of penciled-in dots, a few single strokes, and only a couple of Xs to mark where a task was completed.

Communications systems got a second stroke to form an X. So did weapons systems. Only a single stroke was placed next to the itemized list that included medevac and maintenance recovery. There was much to be done before all the necessary steps for mission readiness were completed.

Bending down to pick up another stone, Toni sent the rock out onto the water like a bullet. *Plop plop plop plop plop plop~splash.*

Toni inhaled then exhaled along with the expanding circles in the water. She flipped the sheet of her notepad and went over the list again.

"Senior Airman Solis?"

Toni turned at the sound of her rank and name. It was still new to her; that attachment of *senior* to her status. Each time she heard it her heart skipped in thudding plops inside her chest.

"They're ready for you, ma'am."

Toni nodded and folded the pages of notes in half like a hotdog, then in half the other way like a hamburger. Making sure the edges were straight, she tucked the pages into her pocket and turned to leave. But not before picking up one more stone and casting it off into the water.

Plop plop plop plop plop~splash.

Her shoulders jerked as the stone sank into the water on the fifth plop. Her eyes scanned the ground, searching for another rock. She wasn't a superstitious woman, not by any stretch. What she was was methodical, regimented, orderly. She knew that running through tactics again and again, thinking through every eventuality, making a list and checking it twice, that was what saved lives on the battlefield.

"Senior Airman?"

With a purse of her lips, Toni abandoned the water and headed back to the base. It was a short walk from the pond to the military post in the village on the east coast of the African continent. The area was relatively safe, but Toni kept sending glances over her shoulder back to where the stone had prematurely sunk.

On the other side of the water was the small Somalian village where she and her team had been deployed for months now. On the bank, she saw people that looked like her. Women with skin the same color as the fertile earth. But where she wore muted fatigues, they wore vibrant skirts. Where her hair was in two lopsided braids that crowned the sides of her head, their hair was woven in tiny, intricate braids that zigged and zagged in precise patterns.

Toni had had one of the village women do her hair once. Only once. They had gushed over her texturized hair, calling her a White woman even though they could have been long-lost cousins. But anyone who wasn't from the country, or even the continent of Africa, was often called white by those born to the land. And that included African Americans. Regardless of whether their ancestral line was mixed with European or not. It was a prejudice Toni had not expected.

Though the country of Somalia was poor, they had all the basic resources necessary, including fertile land, livestock, and fish. But many kept looking west. Toni had had many marriage proposals, a few even forceful despite the uniform on her back and the weapon slung over her shoulder.

Airman Solis wasn't interested in marriage. Her career in the military would be her only beau for the foreseeable future. Her children would be the medals she intended to collect as she rose through the ranks. Men were a distraction that was not included on her list.

Inside TOC, her team was assembled. The

Tactical Operations Center was the hub of the specially trained military personnel on the base. It hummed with a different energy, a seriousness of the dangerous and daring missions the men and women inside these walls were prepared to take. Checking the digital clock on the wall, Toni saw that they had time to run over the mission details one more time before departure.

"We're ready to go." It wasn't a question that Senior Master Sergeant Sinkins posed. He stood with his hands behind his back in an at-ease stance. Though the man was never at ease, he was always at the ready.

"Sir," Toni began, "we have time to run through the details one more—"

"No time for another prep."

Her heart skipped a beat at that voice. Just one skip and then a splash because she knew she could never manage to stay afloat in the presence of a man like him. Which was why she always tried to keep a body of water between them. Which was why she didn't turn to look at him as she spoke.

"A rush through prep is a rush to failure," said Toni.

"We have the element of surprise," said Captain

Topher Matthews in that deep, arrogant baritone of his. "Missions never go exactly as planned. You have to account for the unexpected."

"Not when I plan them," said Toni. "You either learn by mindless repetition or blunt force trauma."

She'd avoided looking at him for almost a whole minute. She could have lasted longer. Instead, he disrupted her plan and came around to stand directly in front of her.

Toni bit her lip to hold in her gasp. No man should be this beautiful. And worse, he knew how good looking he was. Even worse than the worse, he knew the effect his looks had on women.

His golden locks were just a touch too long. His blue eyes were clearer than the skies he loved to fly in. His grin was a flash of white teeth that warned he was a wolf in pilot's clothing.

"You know how to make God laugh?" Matthews snatched the folded notepaper from her hands and held it up. "You make a plan. And that's coming from a preacher's kid."

Matthews liked to throw that in their faces from time to time. As though he was holier than thou, even though he was the biggest womanizer on the base. And the most irresponsible. He hated prep and often went off script while on a mission. But because he always got the task done, he rarely to never was dressed down over his actions.

"Time is of the essence on this mission," said Sinkins, his at-ease stance at full attention now. "Solis, gather your team and head out."

"Yes, sir."

That was the end of the argument. The command was given, and she'd have to obey. It was her favorite thing about being in the military: the orderliness of it. The rank and file of it. Everyone knew where they belonged and what they had to do. If ever there was a question, it was clearly spelled out, or rather barked out, by the person above you.

It was also the thing she hated about the military; the orderliness of it. It meant that a corner cutter like Matthews could pull rank and override her, even if she knew she had the right of it.

She ignored the grin Matthews shot her way, refusing to catch his eye. He just wanted to rub it in that he'd gotten one over on her. He could be childish like that.

Fifteen minutes later, Toni and her unit were in a copter with Matthews at the command. As the aircraft lifted off, she spied the small pond that bordered the base of the village. The waters were still under the cover of night. Nothing skimmed the surface. Not a ripple in sight.

Toni turned her attention back to the mission at hand. This should work. She'd drilled her team enough. She'd thought of every eventuality. They were ready.

Her stomach dropped as the bird went up higher. It was the irony of the decade that she was an airman that got woozy with each takeoff. Especially the way Matthews flew -the show-off.

The aircraft jerked. It wasn't the jerk of acceleration. It was the jerk of an impact.

Lifting her head, she sought Matthews. He had one hand on the yoke, tugging with all his might at the control wheel. But it was to no avail. They were dipping down in dizzying circles.

Matthews sent a glance over his shoulder. His gaze connected with hers. Toni had always avoided looking directly into his eyes, afraid she'd fall like so many women before her. But now, when she looked at those blue eyes, they were the only thing that she could hold on to.

Toni felt like a stone skipping across the skies. One plop. Two plops. She lost count of how many plops there were as they skidded through the air. The sound of the splash on the ground was deafening to her ears.

And then everything went black.

CHAPTER TWO

opher scratched at his chest. The raised bumps he found there irritated him more than the fading bruise below his eye did. He'd had his nose broken many a time in his life. At times because he opened his mouth. At other times because his gaze had strayed to a woman who wasn't as free as her flirtatious gaze let on. But mostly he'd gotten his nose broken in the heat of battle.

The last battle he'd fought had been two months ago. Though the wounds on his body were all but faded, something inside him hadn't healed quite right.

Every time he closed his eyes, he saw it. The bright light of the blast. The inkiness of the dark sky.

The flashing lights of his console. The spark in Toni Solis's eyes that had gone out when he'd lost control of the craft.

For some reason, seeing her fear had kicked him into high gear. He'd managed to land the craft, but not without extensive damage to the copter and those inside. The one who had been injured the worst had been Solis.

Topher had been a fighter all his life. Even before joining the armed forces. He loved as hard as he fought.

Though love was a strong word. The raised skin over his heart agreed with him. Thinking about how it had gotten there had his heart skipping a beat.

The streaks across the sky that had looked like lightning but weren't. The ground coming at him fast. Then black. Then red.

Topher peered in the mirror at the angry scar he'd gotten as he'd climbed over burning metal to get to her. To make sure the fire that was always in her eyes was still there. But her eyes had been closed. Her body was limp and broken.

"You all right there, son?"

Topher snatched the edges of his shirt together, fastening the buttons with quick fingers as he met his father's gaze. He hadn't meant to leave the bedroom door open. He'd only come in to grab a change of shirt after the day's chores on the ranch.

Things were busier than usual on the Flying Cross ranch after the weddings. Both his brother Charlie and his long-time girlfriend Savy and his brother Joe and his first love Foxy had said their vows. Now Charlie and Savy were headed away for their honeymoon. By the time the couple came back, there would be three prefabricated homes on the ranch.

Three because his brother Will had wasted no time in proposing to Tricksy, the girl who had been Topher's first love. Though there was that word again—*love*. It hadn't been love between Topher and Tricksy. At least not on his part.

There had only been one woman he could ever profess to loving. He'd fallen hard for his adoptive mother at the tender age of nine. Tessa Matthews had been everything to the mistrusting foster child that Topher had been. He'd lived for her smiles, happily did the dishes for a hug, and even remembered to always flush the toilet for her winks.

He'd only ever felt emotions like that for her. He couldn't imagine feeling them for any other woman.

He didn't care to. Especially not when the hurt of losing his adopted mom still weighed down his heart.

So, no, Topher hadn't loved Tricksy in the way that she wanted to be loved. The way that Will loved her back when they were kids and now that they were grown adults. But he would be here for their wedding at the end of the month. He'd stay a few days to make sure the homes got delivered. But after that, he needed to decompress, and to do that, he would go camping alone in the wilderness for a few weeks until his next deployment.

But first, he had a mission to complete. "Dad..." he began and stopped.

Topher had never been good at asking for help. He preferred to do everything on his own. Being a burden was what had gotten him thrown into foster care at a young age. He remembered his biological father shouting at his mother that he couldn't afford her and *the kid.* He never called Topher by his name. Even when he went out the door that final time, he'd told his mother he wasn't going to be responsible for her and her kid any longer. A year later, and his mother left and didn't come back.

They were both alive and well. He'd looked them

up while in high school. Topher had vowed never to be too much of a handful to his adoptive parents, not after everything they'd done for him. The request he was about to make wasn't for him. Not exactly.

"Dad," he began again.

"What is it, son?" Father Matthews came into the bedroom, shutting the door behind him. It was as though his father knew he needed privacy to make this request.

"I know we're a bit crowded here on the ranch, but I was wondering if we could make space for one more?"

His father's face was a mask of patience as he regarded his son. Haran Matthews had to know instinctively that there was more to this story than Topher was letting on. Because Topher never asked for anything that he couldn't get for himself.

"Since the guest house will be empty," Topher continued, "I wanted to let a buddy of mine use it while they recover from their injuries."

The scar on Topher's chest itched again, but he stopped himself from scratching at it. *Buddy* was the wrong word. He and his intended guest had never done a buddy thing the entire time they'd known each other. Other than to come out alive after their last mission together. The others on the mission had come out as well. All a bit broken and bruised, but none as banged-up as Solis.

Everyone else had been able to get to their feet and get clear of the crash. She was the only one who'd had to be carried. As he'd picked her up and into his arms, the folded paper with her readiness plan on it had slipped out of her pocket. Before he could grab it, the fire had claimed one edge and consumed the document whole.

"A Wounded Warrior?" asked Father Matthews.

"Yes, Airman Toni Solis."

"Of course, son. Any friend of yours, and any fellow airman, is welcome here." His father gave a nod and headed for the door. "Just let me know when he'll arrive."

Topher gulped, trying to hold down the half-truth he'd just let slip by. The whole truth was that Airman Antonia Solis wasn't a man. Even more of the truth was that it was Topher's fault that she had been injured in the first place.

She'd had a plan. Maybe if he'd followed that plan, maybe if he'd listened, then…

No. That wasn't the way they were trained to think. Things could go wrong in missions, and they had that time. But they'd lived to fight another day.

Topher would do just that. He would go back to the battlefield and fight once more for his country. Just as soon as he got Solis settled.

At least now he had the chance to make it up to her by bringing her here to the ranch to get better.

CHAPTER THREE

Plop plop plop—splash.

Plop plop plop plop—splash.

Toni rubbed the surface of the next rock in her palm. She waited for the waters to settle. The surface of the pond was clear and blue, just like the waters had been back in Somalia. That was unusual for a lot of bodies of waters in the States where things were often polluted from overcrowding and dumping.

If she stared hard, she might see the rock sink to the bottom of the pond. But the blue got darker the deeper she looked. The dark blue reminded her of the sky swirling around her.

Toni shut her eyes. She found no solace behind her eyelids. She stayed awake, eyes wide open, most nights with all the lights on to avoid walking in a nightmare of shadows.

Raising her arm, she let the rock fly. The perpetual twinge in the muscle of her forearm called the throw up short. Her fingers released the stone before her wrist could get the proper flick on it.

Plop plop—splash.

The stone sank instantly, barely causing a ripple. It hadn't skipped far enough to make any real impact. But the impact remained in her forearm and alerted her shoulder that there was something for it to complain about. The wound that had been plaguing her since she'd hit the ground during the crash came to life with all the agitation of tossing the rocks.

She raised her arms out in front of her in a Y shape, like an eagle spreading its wings. Crossing her arms one over the other, she pressed her forearms together in the yoga pose known as The Eagle. She repeated the motion, opening and closing her arms like the proud bird about to take flight.

The relief from the pain was instant. But that's where the relief ended. So long as the injury remained completely unhealed, Toni would not be taking flight any time soon. She was still grounded by the United States military.

It was a temporary setback. She had a plan. Of course she did. So long as she went over every step, she would be ready again. Soon.

There were still rocks on the ground. She reached for one. As she bent down, her left knee wobbled, unprepared to take on more of a load.

Toni managed to grab the rock and not tip over before bringing herself back upright. As she stood to attention, the ache returned. The doctors said it would always be there. No matter how much rehabilitation she did.

Doctors didn't understand her determination.

Rubbing her thumb over the face of the stone, Toni lifted her hand and tossed again. The rock sailed a few feet away from her, gliding over the surface of the calm water before landing with a splutter just off the bank of the pond.

Toni cursed under her breath and knelt down again. Her knee hadn't given out on her. Sometimes the weight of everything she'd been through, everything she'd yet to face, came crashing down on her injured shoulders.

"Senior Airman Solis?"

Toni bristled at the call of her name. During her time at the hospital, she'd been *ma'am* and *soldier*, or even *Ms. Solis* a few times. She missed hearing the rank she'd worked so hard for. She turned to the sound of the voice and was confronted with a metal leg. Looking up, she found Dylan Banks waiting patiently at the end of the pier.

"It's time," said the vet and founder of the Purple Heart Ranch.

Toni carefully put her feet under her. She came to standing with only a wobble. That was the easy part. The first step was a doozy.

"You've done very well during your time here, Toni."

Toni had been skeptical about coming to the rehabilitation ranch. Planting seeds and weeding flowers for dexterity? Caring for animals to help combat PTSD? Turns out there was something to it all. But it was riding horses that had improved the functionality of her injured leg the most.

"Too bad I can't stay and continue my healing," she said.

"You know the rules," said Dylan.

"I'm pretty sure the rules are against the law."

The Purple Heart Ranch was a rehabilitation haven for veterans and Wounded Warriors from all legs of the Armed Services. But a local zoning law indicated that only families could stay and live on the ranch.

That meant that any soldier who came to stay had three months' worth of healing provided at no cost to them. If they wanted to stay longer, the cost would be a marriage license. Meaning they'd have to get hitched. It was a restriction Toni was not willing to abide by.

"No one here's complaining." Dylan had a grin on his face as he looked out at the ranch he'd helped build.

Toni followed the trajectory of his line of sight. In the distance, she saw his pretty wife, Maggie, and their toddler trailing behind her. Maggie threw her head back and laughed as the child tried to keep up with a ragtag pack of dogs. As the woman leaned back with her hands on her low back, her pregnant belly was pronounced in her sundress.

Toni snuck another glance at Dylan. The pride and love were so bright in his eyes that Toni had to divert her gaze. She had one memory of her mother's smile. She had none of her father.

Smiling moms and dads were plentiful here on the Purple Heart Ranch. Toni had met a number of the couples, and they all looked happy. Happy with each other. Happy with their offspring. It was unfamiliar territory for Toni, and she wouldn't be too sad about leaving the anomalous terrain. Soon, she would be heading back into the military to reclaim the career that made her proud.

She would miss this place, though. She'd grown up in the city. Not the inner city. Just a nice suburb adjacent to a big city.

She'd been raised by a single dad after her mom passed away when Toni was just eight years old. Her dad had never remarried. He'd never even dated again, as far as Toni could tell. He was married to his career and had little time or attention to give to another woman... and that included his own daughter.

At the end of the drive, Toni saw a golden-haired man who was getting a lot of attention. A small group of women surrounded him. They all grinned up at him with little cartoon hearts in their eyes.

Toni rolled her eyes at the display. When she brought her gaze back around to the scene, Topher Matthews's eyes weren't on any of his admirers. Those baby blues were locked on her.

Matthews had walked away from the crash that had put her career on hold. He'd walked away with only a scratch on his chest, where her body was banged up and bruised. But she'd been told that he'd walked away from the crash carrying her in his arms. If he hadn't done that, she would be dead.

And now he was coming to rescue her again.

Her time at the Purple Heart Ranch was up. She could've gone to her father's home, but he had moved into a one-bedroom apartment recently which was a hundred miles away from the nearest VA hospital. She needed to be near a clinic to continue her rehab so that she could get cleared to go back into active duty. Which left Matthews as her only option.

Not that she'd asked him for his help. He'd offered. She'd opened her mouth to refuse, but nothing came out. She'd meant to ask for details, for facts and figures, at least a direction so she'd know where she'd be going. For the first time in her life, she was stepping forward without a plan in place.

Hopefully, this was the way to get God to stop laughing at her.

CHAPTER FOUR

She looked thinner than before. Or maybe that's because Topher had never seen Toni Solis out of her fatigues.

He had to blink and turn away at that thought. He'd never had one like it before, seeing Solis out of uniform. He'd never thought of her like that, like a woman.

Of course, he knew she was a woman. He'd simply always thought of her as a soldier. One of the best. If a little too regimented and analytical for his liking.

Solis was as straight-laced as they came. Except for her hair. For a woman who liked to line up everything nicely, the parts in her hair were almost always askew and crooked.

That included today. The two braids woven around her head like a crown were uneven, one higher on her head than the other. The other was lower but thicker, as though she was off balance.

He liked it. Liked seeing Little Miss Perfect, Little Ms. Orderly in some form of disarray. That wasn't the only thing he was noticing about her.

She wore a T-shirt and jeans that hugged her curves. Curves that had always been hidden beneath the baggy uniform. Curves that were now on display as he looked his fill.

Beside him, he heard the distant notes of feminine chatter and giggles. He'd completely forgotten about the girls that had been flirting with him while he waited for Solis. He left them standing and met Solis at the back of his truck.

She avoided his gaze. Looking down. Looking up. Looking everywhere but at him.

"You ready?" he asked.

All he got was a bob of her head. The nodding gesture was canted a little to the left, the side where the braid was thicker. His gaze caught and held on the tight curls that had escaped the weaving.

He caught her looking at him then. Her gaze narrowed, and she frowned. She ducked her head, but not before running a self-conscious hand over her hair.

Topher had parked in front of the small cabin she'd been staying in. On the porch were bags. Solis was headed for them, but he beat her.

"I can do it myself," she said, brushing past him.

But her brushing past him was a couple of limping steps. Topher halted in indecision. He knew Solis was one of the best, but he'd seen her go down. He'd tasked himself with picking her back up. Seeing the bright light go out of those eyes, holding her limp body in his arms as he raced to get her to safety, had shaken him.

Topher wanted nothing more than to see the female soldier back in her top form. But that limp told him that she wasn't there yet. The wince when she hefted the bags up and onto her shoulder screamed that she needed help.

Topher looked at Dylan, who pursed his lips. Dylan gave a slight shake of his head, but his eyes remained watchful of Solis's every move, as though he was prepared to jump in if the load became too much for her. Topher followed that cue.

Like all Matthews men, Topher loved a strong woman. His adoptive mother had been tough as nails. Tessa Matthews had had to be to wrangle six high energy boys. But Tessa had been strong enough to let a man do things for her. Solis was a violently independent woman, one who Topher had witnessed bite a man's head off if he dared offer to carry her gear for her. So opening the car door was likely the wrong step, too.

Balling his hands into fists and putting them behind his back, Topher watched her struggle with the bags as she dumped them into the bed of the truck. It went against everything he'd been taught by his father to let a woman struggle. But Solis was a military woman, and Topher knew how important it was for women warriors to be seen as equal.

He stepped around the car to the passenger side door. He knew he'd catch it by opening it for her, but he would take this heat.

She didn't look up at him as he held the door open for her. Once she was safely inside, he shut her in, feeling panic rise in him. They'd be in the truck for over an hour as they headed back to the Flying Cross Ranch. What would they talk about?

Hopefully not that last mission that had left her wounded and her military career in shambles. He was set to head back in less than a month, where she couldn't be on her own yet. Which was why he was picking her up.

Topher turned and thanked Dylan. The man sent him off with a *good luck.*

When he climbed into the car, Solis was sitting rigid in the passenger seat like the soldier she was. Her gaze was trained out the window. Her lips pursed.

In her hand was a stone. She rubbed at the smooth surface, reminding him of a gambler rubbing at dice. He knew she had a habit of skipping stones. He wanted to tell her that there was a creek on the ranch. He wanted to tell her that he'd skipped stones there as a kid. But all those were personal matters, and he never discussed details like that with women. It gave them the wrong idea.

The women who'd been flirting with him watched with pouts as he pulled away from the curb. Clearly, they had the wrong idea about him and Solis. They weren't a couple. They weren't even friends. But he felt responsible for her, which was why he was taking her home to heal.

The Purple Heart Ranch had done as much for her as the place could. But on the Flying Cross Ranch, with the strength and guidance of his father, Solis would be as good as new in no time. If that ranch could turn around six wild foster boys, it could easily heal one wounded woman.

He'd drop her off. Make sure she was settled with his dad looking over her. Then he'd be on his way, his debt to her repaid. With that plan in place, Topher settled back into the long drive.

"You're a cowboy?" said Solis, breaking the silence. "Why doesn't that surprise me?"

"I wasn't born on a ranch. I grew up in the inner city."

Solis looked at him as though he was lying. She had the most judgmental eyes. But at least the spark was back in them. Her eyes were the color of coffee, his favorite beverage. Coffee never judged. It gave energy and comfort and strength. All of a sudden, Topher found himself very thirsty.

"I'm the product of an affair," Topher found himself saying. "My mother tried to use me to get my father to leave his wife. He stayed for a while, but then he went back to his family. She left shortly after he did."

"She just left you with other family members?"

"No, she left me completely alone in the apartment. I stayed until the landlord came looking for rent. By then, I'd eaten all the food and was starving."

"How old were you?"

"Five."

Topher had no idea why he told her this. He was

never this chatty with women. He would always get them talking as he found a way to steer them back to their room or his. He wasn't steering Solis anywhere. She was coming home with him to live on the ranch. So it didn't count.

"What about you? Your mother was in the Army?"

"She was."

Topher waited for her to add more. Women always filled silences with chatter. Not Solis. "She retired?"

"She died. Not combat related."

"So your dad raised you?"

Solis shrugged. "I pretty much raised myself. My dad was a workaholic. I was a latchkey kid since first grade."

"That explains it."

Her head whipped to him. "Explains what?"

"Your independence."

"You say that like it's a bad thing."

"People need people."

"Look, you don't have to worry about me. I mean, I appreciate you letting me crash at your place. But I won't overstay my welcome. It should just be a few weeks more of rehab at the VA. Then I'm applying for reinstatement."

Topher pursed his lips. Her injuries were severe.

He knew that for certain. He'd held her broken body in his arms. She was one of the best strategists he'd ever worked with. But he wasn't so sure about that timeline.

It wasn't going to be his problem. He'd drop her off. Get her settled in the guest house. Then he'd be off soon.

CHAPTER FIVE

It was blessedly quiet on the drive. But Toni was still tense. It wasn't that she didn't trust Matthews behind the wheel. The man had flown an aircraft in a war zone with heavy enemy fire that had taken them down, and still he'd managed to get them on the ground with their lives.

They were on a country road, not in contested airspace. Their only adversaries were the deer dotting the lines of the forest. The occasional herd of cows busied themselves in the rolling pastures. In the distance, wild horses ran fast and free, their manes streaking behind them.

Toni turned in her seat to watch as the horses ran past. Her eyes were big, her mouth slightly open. In her hand, she'd taken the stone out of her pocket and was rubbing at the smooth surface of the rock. Her heavy limbs felt weightless as she watched the beasts run. Her heartbeat picked up as they disappeared over the horizon.

She caught Matthews's gaze on her, and her heart thumped. She turned back around in her seat and faced forward. The weight resettled in her limbs.

Matthews didn't say anything, and she was grateful. The honk of a truck idling down the road caught his attention. With a closed fist, he pounded the center of the steering wheel, giving off a short, friendly beep.

She eyed those hands. Her mind flashed back to how he'd held on to the yoke in the aircraft back in Somalia. When the next truck zoomed past them at the speed limit, Toni's entire body tensed.

She pinched the skin at her throat when Matthews got too close to the edge of the shoulder. She tugged at the edge of her braid each time he took his hand off the steering wheel to reach for his bottled water. She nearly had a heart attack when he reached for the stereo dial.

"You can choose," he said.

"Beg pardon?"

"The tunes," he said, resettling his hand on the steering wheel. "You can choose what we listen to."

Toni let loose a slow exhale. She had to unfurl her fingers from the seatbelt before she could reach for the radio dial. So much of her life had been out of her control for the last three months. From the time she'd lost in a coma while on a base hospital for nearly two weeks. To the time at the Purple Heart Ranch where she wasn't sure if she would walk unassisted again.

She was so used to being in control that her brain was having trouble functioning. Reaching for the dial, she turned the knob too far in one direction when she knew that tuning into any one station was done in small turns. When a familiar tune hit her ears, Toni stopped the twisting of the dial. She settled back against the headrest and let out another sigh.

A baritone voice that she didn't remember from the song hit her ears with the melody. Toni opened her eyes and glanced over at Matthews. Sure enough, his lips were moving, and it was his voice singing the lyrics.

"You know Mahalia Jackson?" she asked.

"Of course I do." When the look of shock didn't leave her face, he continued, "I told you, I'm a preacher's kid."

It was still hard for her to believe that Topher

Matthews was even a child of God, much less that he could actually go into a church without being smitten down. The man had broken so many hearts, many at the same time.

Mahalia Jackson crooned on about helping somebody as she traveled along. The gospel singer's voice had always felt like a warm blanket to Toni's ears. She reached to turn the volume up. At the same time, Matthews was reaching for the knob. Their fingers brushed.

Toni couldn't hide her gasp. A zing from her index finger spread through her palms. From there, warmth spread through her entire body, making her shiver with the impact of it.

"You cold?" he asked, completely unaffected. His long fingers moved from the volume and reached instead for the AC dial.

There was no need to. Toni's entire body felt like it was on fire. She tugged at her braids again, wishing that her hair was long enough to hide her face.

She shifted in the seat. It was difficult for her to sit for long periods of time. Her leg was already cramping, her knee threatening a tantrum if she kept it cooped up much longer. But she needed to get out of this car and away from close proximity to

Matthews as quickly as possible. That meant staying put as they drove to their destination. So she didn't complain.

When Topher turned the wheel and pulled off at the next exit, she opened her mouth to protest, but her foot was too busy tapping at the floorboards. Her body was far too eager for a reprieve to let any words escape.

"Hope you don't mind," he said as he parked the car. "Just need to stretch my legs a bit."

Toni eyed the man as he got out of the truck. She eyed his long, lithe body that moved with ease and power. She watched as his powerful legs carried him to the front of the car without a wobble or a misstep.

Matthews raised his arms over his head and stretched his big body. A sliver of golden tan skin was exposed as he did so. Toni couldn't take her eyes off the spot. She wasn't the only one.

A few other women scattered around the rest stop were enjoying the show. Some covertly sneaking gazes as they looked past the men or children talking to them. A few overtly as they flipped their long hair over their shoulders and tugged at pouty lips.

Matthews grinned at them as he brought his arms down. Emboldened, or invited, a couple of the women came over, boobs first. Toni swore that each of those girls had somehow lowered her T-shirt the moment she stepped up beside Matthews.

Toni curled her lip as she reached for the handle and shoved the passenger door open. Matthews glanced at her as he continued to speak to the women. The women didn't look over at her, not even eying Toni as competition.

She wasn't competition. She certainly didn't want to be in the running for that man's heart. Or any man's heart. She was on a mission.

She would crash at the Matthews ranch, go to the VA to continue her rehab, and then get reinstated. That was the plan. Those were the check boxes on her list. That was all that mattered.

She stepped out of the vehicle, but her leg wasn't ready. When her heel impacted the ground, she stumbled. The top half of her body pitched forward. She held out her hands to brace herself, but her palms never hit the dirt.

Strong arms came around her. Those arms caught her forearms and lifted her upright. Toni looked up to find Matthews's face close to hers.

Her hand was against his chest. On the warm flesh just inside his button-up shirt. There were more than a few buttons undone, which allowed her index finger to rest on raised skin.

She knew he had come away with a scratch. Was that it? Right over his heart?

Matthews set her away from him. Then he reached up to his shirt and yanked the buttons through their holes, closing up his shirt and hiding his wound.

"Let me know when you're ready," he said in his gruff voice. Then he walked away from her.

CHAPTER SIX

Topher kept an eye on Solis's leg. Her left leg was closer to him, though he knew it was the right one that had sustained the injury. Both looked shapely encased in the denim of her jeans. Long and lean with a dainty foot encased in dark running shoes. He wanted to remove the shoes and replace them with boots. He'd bet a pair of cowboy boots would make her impossibly long legs even longer and accentuate the curves of her hips.

Realizing he was checking out her shapely thighs and making plans for her curves, Topher averted his gaze.

He didn't know what to do with this woman. Any evidence he showed of trying to care for her needs was met with haughty suspicion. If he feigned igno-rance, he was dealt a twisted curl of her lip.

What was he supposed to do?

All he knew to do was to get her to the ranch. His father would know what to do. His father could fix anything. Haran Matthews could heal any wound, whether it be physical or emotional. Solis clearly had both.

He'd seen her try to hide every wince of pain as the truck bumped over dips in the road. It was why he'd kept to the speed limit on their drive, even though it was evident she was having trouble on the long ride. Her mouth had remained mute, but each tightening of her lips, every narrowing of her eyes, he'd caught.

Topher knew how to dress a physical wound. He had military training for it. He also had five brothers who'd roughhoused as kids and young adults and needed to hide the evidence of any wound from their parents.

There was nothing he could do for her leg or shoulder. She wouldn't even let him lift her luggage. And he sure as all the hay in the world didn't know what to do with an emotional wound. Which is what girls seemed to get most of the time.

Most times, to heal something on the inside required words. He was known as a smooth talker, but those coffee dark eyes of hers had met any of his words today with a bitter glare that left a foul taste on his tongue.

Solis wasn't one to be charmed. And if a man couldn't charm a woman, then what was he supposed to do with her?

Didn't matter. He didn't need to answer that question. His father would handle it.

Though there was a slight problem with that plan. Topher hadn't told his father that Toni Solis was a woman.

It wasn't a lie.

He'd just neglected to correct his dad when he'd made the assumption that the gender neutral name belonged to a woman and not a man.

Topher knew Father Matthews would take her in. He was like that. The man had taken in six wild boys. Though he and his wife had opted not to take in the three James girls who had also been in foster care with his foster brothers.

Topher had always assumed that was because Savy and Charlie had declared they were in love with each other before they'd reached double digits in age. He later learned it was because the girls' parents refused to relinquish their parental rights, even though the drug addicts kept coming close to having their rights terminated with each passing year that they didn't straighten up. By the time the drugs did the James adults in, Savy was legal and took on the care of her two younger sisters herself.

And now, with the old foster home being demolished and moved to the bunkhouse of the Flying Cross Ranch, Haran Matthews had taken in the adult James women and their five foster kids. At least he was bringing his dad a grown woman to fix.

His father would use his booming preacher voice, give Solis the words of wisdom she needed to hear, and the soldier would be back on her feet in no time. Topher's debt to her would be repaid with the only currency he had—his father's love. Because lord knows Topher didn't have any love to give himself.

At last, he pulled into the lane that lead to the Flying Cross Ranch. His heart sighed at the sight of his home. His brothers and their neighbors, the Silver sisters, had made great progress on the new additions. Three of his brothers had decided to come back home and live with their wives.

The prefab homes were settled on new foundations. One was painted red brick, another white, and the third was a riot of colors. That one belonged to the clairsentient Foxy and his straight-laced brother Joe, who'd just given up a chance at being appointed DA in favor of working with state foster kids.

With his brothers and their wives and wife-to-be getting settled in the new houses, that left the guest house available for Toni. Topher pulled up to the main house first. There he saw his father sitting on the porch in his old rocking chair.

"There's my boy," Father Matthews said as he came to standing.

Topher wasn't a boy. But any time this man used that term, a sheepish grin spread over his face. Father Matthews opened his arms, and Topher came into them.

"Hey, Dad."

"I thought you were off to pick up your friend Toni."

"I'm Toni." Solis waved from the side of the truck. She'd hung back, looking uncomfortable at the display of emotions between father and son.

Father Matthews looked at Solis, who bit her lip. Then at Topher, who fixed his gaze on the old barn. It looked like the roof needed some work. The old man shook his head and then offered Solis a bright smile.

"Welcome to the Flying Cross Ranch," said Father Matthews.

"Thank you for having me, sir. I promise I won't be a bother, and I'll be out of your hair as soon as possible."

Father Matthews looked Solis up and down. Topher wasn't sure if she saw it, but his father had taken her number right then and there.

"You stay as long as you need," said Father Matthews.

That had gone easier than Topher had imagined.

"Of course you'll stay in the guest house, while my son stays in the main house," Father Matthews continued. "Forgive me, but I am—how do you kids say it? Old school."

"Oh, no." Solis held up her hand. "No, no, no." She flicked her fingers between herself and Topher. "There's nothing going on between Matthews and me."

As though to make certain it was definitively clear, she made a slicing motion with her hands as though severing the very idea of the two of them in a relationship.

"She needs a place to stay that's close to the VA

hospital," said Topher. "And she's been doing well with equine therapy, so I thought you could give her some lessons."

"Horses?" said Solis. "You didn't say you had horses."

There was an almost smile on her face. Topher got lost a minute in that wide-eyed gaze of hers. He suddenly remembered just how thirsty he was for a hot, large drink of coffee.

"I'd be happy to give you lessons," said Father Matthews. "We can start when I get back."

"When you get back?" Topher jerked to attention, like hot coffee had spilled on his chest.

"I'm away for the long weekend. Charlie and Savy insisted I come on their honeymoon cruise with them."

"You're going on your son's honeymoon cruise?" asked Solis.

"I'm not going to say no to a cruise. And I like my son and his wife."

Solis pursed her lips, as though she tasted something foul or unfamiliar. But she didn't say anything.

Father Matthews turned to Topher. "You can see to her riding lessons during that time."

"Me?"

"You're an excellent rider and teacher. Why not you?"

Because he'd planned to drop her and go on a solo camping trip before his next deployment. But it looked like he was stuck with her.

No good deed goes unpunished, right?

CHAPTER SEVEN

Stairways were her nemesis, with steps being the villain's minions. Toni had learned that there was a difference between steps and stairs. Stairs was the plural of stairway. A stairway was a structure made up of individual risers, or steps, that moved a person upwards.

It was an important distinction for someone who had mobility issues. If she had to climb stairs, meaning multiple stairways, then it was something she wanted to be prepared for. However, if there were just a few steps to climb, her mind and her body wouldn't hold too much tension as she faced the arduous task. But at the end of the day, whether it be stairs or steps, the whole point was to carry the person upwards.

There were only a few steps up and into the guest house. Toni placed her uninjured leg on the first riser. Bending that knee, she lifted her injured left leg onto the next step. Slowly, she straightened that left knee, wincing not from pain but from the *snap, crackle, and popping* sounds her knee made -and was likely to make for the rest of her life.

She only let the full weight of her body rest on her left leg for a split second before calling on the right leg to lift her up onto the last step. Letting out a sigh, she looked over her shoulder at the hill she'd just climbed. There had been a time in her life where she had scaled mountains at a fast clip without taking any rest stops or breathing too heavily.

Those days were in the past. But she still had a bright future ahead of her. She just needed to stick to the plan. A cloud moved over her head, but it was only there for a second.

Once she was inside the guest house, she shut the door behind her, leaving Matthews on the other side. She'd felt his stare on her back as she climbed the steps. Luckily, he hadn't come over to help her. But a glance out the door's window told her that he might be questioning that decision. His handsome face was pinched.

Had he expected her to let him in? Was this offer

a place to stay just some ploy to try to romance her? Toni let out a laugh at that notion.

A glance in the mirror hanging on the wall just inside the door told her that that was a joke. She was not Matthews's type. Though she knew he dabbled with female soldiers from time to time, he preferred civilians. As a lot of committed bachelor soldiers did. They could get in and out with little to no excuses aside from the major one: *Sorry, babe, but I'm being deployed. Duty to country.*

Sometimes that was true. Often it was a lie. A lie women who hung out at bars around the base bought because they just wanted to land a soldier. Just another reason Toni happily neglected her love life.

She loved the career she'd chosen, and she was anxious to get back to it.

As though it heard her heart's desire, her leg throbbed. She'd been inside Matthews' truck for far too long. The stopover had helped, but she needed to stretch it out.

Looking around the guest house, she saw that there was an embroidered rug she could use for stretching in front of the wooden coffee table. The place was done up cozy. It was clear that it had a woman's touch. But there were masculine accents, as though a woman had lived here and thought a man was coming to stay.

Clearly Matthews's father had been expecting a male buddy of his son's to arrive. Toni had seen as much in those bright hazel eyes when they'd landed on her. He'd been surprised, but not angry.

She'd felt the urge to apologize to him for the inconvenience. To promise that she wouldn't be a bother, wouldn't even make a sound. She'd clean up behind herself, so he'd have no cause to be annoyed at her presence.

But Mr. Matthews, or rather Father Matthews, as he'd told Toni to call him, was headed out. That was something Toni was used to. Her father was forever married to his job and never around. But his presence always hung huge in his house. Even in her closet of a bedroom that he'd turned into a home office the day after she'd enlisted.

A knock at the door had Toni turning around. Had Matthews changed his mind? Was he coming inside to press his suit? She was probably the only woman around for miles.

Toni quickly disabused herself of that notion. Not because of the ridiculousness of Topher Matthews being attracted to a woman like her.

Because there were three beauties crowding the doorway.

The women had tanned skin, as though they were of mixed heritage. Their springy, dark hair was at all lengths. The tallest had a halo of soft curls around her head. The shortest one had her hair cut into a bob that bounced around her heart-shaped face, while the one in the middle had her hair pulled back into a tight bun, but a couple of tendrils wrapped around the base of her neck.

When Toni opened the door, she realized she'd miscounted. Coming up to mid-height of the women was a young girl. This fourth member of the group was clearly of African descent with her coca-colored skin. Her hair was done in neat cornrows, making the girl look like a little princess. Toni took a moment to envy the hairstyle, especially the evenly parted rows of braids that were all ruler straight. Toni ran a self-conscious hand over the messy part in her hair.

"Hi, you must be Toni," said the tallest woman. She had a deep baritone of a voice. "I'm Savy, and these are my sisters Foxy and Tricksy."

The names took Toni back. Were these women performers? Or were their parents just on something when they named their kids?

"And this here is LaTisha."

The young girl eyed Toni with the open curiosity of a child. Her gaze went above Toni's eyes to her hairline. LaTisha frowned, but she didn't say anything.

"We just wanted to welcome you," Savy continued. "And make sure you have everything you need before we head out."

Savy pushed her way past Toni as she spoke. The other two women and little girl walked single file behind their leader into the house. They weren't slight women. But Toni was a highly trained soldier. Yet, with her injury, even little LaTisha might get the best of her.

"I'm headed on my honeymoon with Charlie, that's Topher's brother, and his dad."

That bit of information hadn't registered when Toni had heard it the first time outside with Matthews and his dad. Now that it was confirmed, she had to give a shake of her head. Not only was the dad not mad for the unexpected visitor plopped down on his property, but he was going on his kid's honeymoon? What a weird family.

"Foxy is going to be running around with her husband Joe while he does some legal work for state foster kids."

Foxy, the one with the short bob, gave a wave and an apologetic grin.

"But Tricksy will be here to watch over the foster kids."

Tricksy was the only one that, along with LaTisha, hadn't offered Toni a friendly smile. Where LaTisha eyed Toni with child-like curiosity, Tricksy eyed Toni with wary suspicion.

Danger bells should have been ringing in Toni's head. This woman clearly looked at her as an adversary. But for what? It was the first time Toni had met the woman. What did she have against her?

Something else registered louder in Toni's mind. "Foster kids?"

"Didn't Topher tell you?" said Tricksy. "There are five fosters living here."

Toni's gaze landed again on LaTisha. The kid held Toni's stare. Her parents had given her up? Yet she looked so clean and tidy with her pressed clothes and straight cornrows.

"Did he tell you he was a foster kid himself?" asked Tricksy, suspicion oozing from her tone. Her lower lip curled in cynicism. Or was that jealousy?

Toni's gaze dipped to the woman's hands. It was instinct for her to look for a weapon when faced with an adversary. What Toni found on Tricksy's left hand confused her more. There was a sparkling engagement ring on her fourth finger.

"There's nothing between Matthews and me." Toni made an emphatic gesture with her hands, slicing the air. "I needed a place to stay near the VA hospital. He feels guilty for crashing. So here I am."

The three women winced. Toni felt only a slight pang of guilt for speaking about the crash in such a callous manner. But she knew what she'd signed up for, and she wanted to get back to it. Even with the danger she knew it presented. With all its faults, the military had been the only place that had accepted her without conditions.

"We're just glad you're all safe," said Savy, breaking the tense silence.

"Just don't get back on the horse too soon," said Foxy.

Toni wasn't going to listen to that bit of advice. Horseback riding was the one thing that had sent her recovery off the charts. Matthews had promised her a ride, and she was going to take him up on it.

"I can see you're not going to listen to me," Foxy was saying. "When your heart gets thrown, know it's okay to let Topher catch it."

Toni wanted to balk. Matthews hadn't caught her the first time. He was the one who'd made her fall.

She definitely had no intentions of falling for him in the emotional sense. But she fixed her face and showed her manners. Luckily, Savy quickly ushered all the women out of the house with an apologetic smile cast Toni's way.

Such a weird family. They didn't have to worry about Toni overstaying her welcome. As soon as she got better, she'd be out of here on her next deployment.

opher walked the property line. In the distance, he could see the white-capped mountains. A mix of sky-blue and forest-green clashed all around him as nature made its mark on the vista.

Outside of this land, he always felt the need to rush and go as fast as possible, push himself as far as possible. But when here on the Flying Cross Ranch, he felt as though everything around him stood still. And so could he.

He also saw that the ranch needed repairs. The roof of the big house showed wear and tear since they'd last replaced it ten years ago, before they'd all been at home together. When he and his brothers all lived here, everything was in tiptop shape. But they'd all been gone for so long. Because they were all around the same age, there had been a mass exodus. That move had left their father high and dry, the recent victim of a heart attack because he worked himself so hard to maintain his home, their home.

Topher's hand curled into a fist. His father had given him so much. He would not be the man he'd become without him. He probably wouldn't be here on this earth without Haran Matthews.

Luckily, three of his brothers were back home for good. Charlie, Joe, and Will could help keep the place in good form. Topher wasn't ready to settle down. He didn't think he'd ever be. He didn't see why he ever would need to be. But while he was here, he would get as much work done as possible.

This was his home base. It would always be. Whenever he needed to stop, whenever he needed a moment to breathe, whenever he needed to retreat from the world, he'd come back here for a spell before zooming off again.

Three days was a fair price to pay to hold still while his father got a well-deserved vacation. He could do work on the farm and get Solis off to a good start for her rehab.

"Is that a pig up there in the sky?"

"No, I think it's hell freezing over."

Topher rolled his eyes at the sounds of his brothers' voices. He knew what was coming. So he steeled himself for the punches they would swing.

"It must be," said Charlie, "because I never thought I'd see the day that Christopher Matthews brought a girl home."

Topher ducked his brother's jab. Then threw one of his own. It was two against one as Joe snuck up behind him. Those were not fair odds... for his two brothers.

Joe went for a body check. Topher side-stepped the man and got in a shot at Charlie's side. That left his two opponents tending to their wounds while Topher did a Mohammed Ali style dance away from them.

Except Topher hadn't seen Will come up behind him. Will wrapped an arm around Topher's neck and took him down. The brothers rolled on the ground, both trying to gain the upper hand.

At one point, they switched sides. Joe, always angling to get the scales of justice to balance, dove onto Will. Charlie, loyal to the end, took that opportunity to reengage Topher.

It was utter chaos. But that was the Matthews boys.

"I can't wait to meet the woman who's finally

tamed The Topher Matthews," said Will as he brushed dirt from his pants. Unfortunately, that grass stain would live on those pants from now on.

"It's not like that," said Topher, swiping at his bottom lip and coming away with blood. He wiped the fluid on his pants and came to standing, unperturbed.

"You told Dad she was a man."

Topher shrugged. "Sometimes I forget Solis is a woman."

Though he hadn't when he'd seen her this morning on the Purple Heart Ranch. Not in those jeans that hugged curves he'd never known were there. Not when she'd leaned her head against the passenger-side window as the sun's rays had kissed her brown skin.

"Yeah, right," said Charlie. "I caught a glimpse of her on the way here. She's definitely all woman."

"Shut it, or I'll tell Savy," said Topher, throwing out another jab, which Charlie ducked.

"Tell my wife whatever you want. She knows she has me wrapped around her little finger."

"And she knows you like it," said Joe.

Charlie grinned wide in confirmation.

"Solis needs help," said Topher, ignoring his

brother's antics. "Dad always says to help each other."

In a chorus that their musical wives would've appreciated, all three of his brothers snorted.

"I'm sure you were going to help her," said a feminine voice. "That's why you were about to drop her and run."

Topher tried not to groan, but he couldn't hide his wince. For years, anytime he came face to face with Tricksy James, he steeled himself for the blow that would inevitably land square on his nose.

Like all the James girls, Tricksy knew how to fight dirty. But she didn't come to Topher. She went into Will's arms. Still, that didn't mean she wasn't coming for him.

Tricksy had fancied herself in love with Topher for more than half her life. She'd even written a song about it that had become a popular breakup anthem on the local charts. Though he hadn't heard her singing it lately. Topher supposed he had Will to thank for that.

Will Matthews had been in love with Tricksy for longer than Tricksy had thought herself in love with Topher. It had taken a little white lie for the two of them to finally see the truth that had been right in front of them all along.

What the two of them had was real, Topher knew that beyond a shadow of a doubt. He could spot love. Enough to know that he wanted little to nothing to do with it.

He'd seen how his birth had contributed to the loss of his biological father, who had been and still remained married. He'd seen how the loss of his adoptive mother had affected his dad. He'd felt the loss himself. Still felt it. Topher didn't want anyone to have that kind of power over him.

"I wasn't trying to drop her and run," he said. But looking around at his brothers' faces, he saw he had no support. Because everyone knew that had been his ultimate plan. "Dad's good at this stuff. So is Savy. Solis is in better hands with them."

"Any woman is in better hands so long as they're not yours." And with that, Tricksy gave Will a passionate kiss, a wink, and walked off.

Will looked stupidly at her as she walked away. Then he turned to glance at Topher. "You know you're going to have to fix that."

Topher sighed. Another reason he'd planned to drop off Solis and get out of here. Everyone kept insisting that he and Tricksy have a talk. Topher hated having talks, especially when they were about feelings. It was why he didn't do relationships.

He wasn't even in a relationship with Tricksy, but to make his family happy, he'd have to sit down and have a talk about their feelings. Or rather, she would. Because he didn't have any feelings on the matter. He didn't think she should have any feelings left for him now that she was with Will.

But to make everyone around him happy, he'd do it. He'd just let her yell at him until she tired herself out. Then his dad and Savy would be back. And he could go off on a solo camping trip. Then he would leave for his deployment. And that would be that.

CHAPTER NINE

*T*oni woke to silence as the sun's rays crept into the bedroom. The bright light trod a muted path across the sheets on the bed. Nothing stirred, not even the dust motes in the air. The hushed stillness reminded her of her childhood.

It was always quiet in her father's house. Either he came home late after she'd already made herself a microwave dinner and went to bed. Or he was gone early in the morning before she got herself up and dressed, toasted a Pop Tart, and made her way to school.

Most days, they talked through notes left for each other on the kitchen counter. His notes were always short, quickly scrawled, and barely legible. There wasn't much Toni had to communicate with him about. He'd given her permission to forge his signature on permission slips as soon as she'd learned cursive writing. If he'd ever signed something of importance himself, the school administration would definitely have thought his autograph was the forgery.

In the military, it was never quiet. Definitely not on the base. There was always motion or action. Or snoring. Or farting. Or low conversations over electronic devices to loved ones in different time zones.

Toni had loved every minute of it. Loved the shards of light that always seemed to shine at every minute of the day and night. Loved the frequency of the sounds—no matter how vulgar. She had never been alone on base. And there was always someone looking out for her.

Here, on the Flying Cross Ranch, all Toni could hear was the sound of the wind rustling leaves. Even the chickens were relatively quiet. She rolled out in the comfortable bed and prepared for the day. It was early in the morning, just after dawn, but she saw she wasn't the only one up.

Five kids moved about the ranch. There was a mix of boys and girls. They were of differing heights, which told her they were a range of ages. They were also of differing races, by the looks of the hues of the skin tones ranging from the brown-skinned LaTisha to a little girl who was just a touch too pale for someone clearly used to working outdoors.

The children moved about the farm carrying pales, moving bales of hay, and tossing out feed to the penned-in animals. What Toni didn't see were any adults around them. Were the Matthewses running a child labor farm here?

No. She doubted that. Not when all the kids wore grins on their faces as they went about their chores.

"Thought you'd sleep in."

Toni's heart slammed against her chest at the sound of Matthews's voice. It wasn't easy to sneak up on her. Especially not for this man whose location she made sure to always know when they were in a room together.

"Training," she said, turning to face him.

Looking directly at his face was a mistake. He'd let his blond mane of hair grow wild since he'd been off base. And by wild, she meant there was a good two inches of locks radiating around his face. She felt overheated gazing up at him.

Matthews nodded as though he didn't need her to expound on that one-word answer that she'd given. They'd had the same training. His more extensive than hers because he'd been in the Air Force longer and had risen higher.

"You want breakfast first? Or do you want to get started?" Matthews asked.

"Started?"

"With your rehab."

"I don't have a VA appointment until Monday."

"I know," he said, stepping closer.

Instinct warned her to step back. Everyone knew what happened to those who flew too close to the sun. Instead, she held still, letting his warmth seep into her aching limbs.

"I was going to take you out for a ride. Equine therapy worked on your leg."

Toni perked up at that, an unguarded smile starting at the corner of her mouth. She'd loved riding on the horses at the Purple Heart Ranch. Sitting atop the majestic beasts had restored some of the power she'd lost after the crash.

"Yes, please."

Matthews's grin was like a heatwave. It singed the hair on her forearms yet still managed to leave behind goosebumps. It was the heart-stopping grin she saw him give to other women.

Toni crossed her arms over her shoulders. "I

mean, yes, that would be agreeable. If it's not too much trouble."

"No trouble at all. I want you well."

Of course he did. Because he wanted her out of here and out of his hair. Well, he'd get that soon, sooner if she could help it.

He held out his hand in a gesture for her to precede him. She took a deep breath and braced herself for the descent down the three steps. Down was always harder than up.

Though she took that deep breath, there was nothing to actually brace herself with. No handrail to lean on. All that was there was Matthews's strong bicep, which she refused to reach for.

She stepped down onto the first step with her good leg. That meant her injured knee only need carry her full weight once for the second step. Toni transferred the weight quickly, but she couldn't hold back the grunt of pain.

She glanced over at Matthews, but he was looking away from her, his face turned off into the distance. But Toni caught sight of the tension in his jaw. When she looked down, she saw both his hands clenched into fists.

His body relaxed once they were on level ground. He kept his pace slow as they headed to the barn.

Toni tried to go double pace. Partly to show him she didn't need coddling. Mostly because she was eager to get to the horses.

"This is Mahalia," he said as he brought out a beautiful black mare. "She's been with us since I was a boy."

Toni couldn't imagine Matthews as a boy. She couldn't see this majestic beast as a pony. Like all females, the horse nuzzled at Matthews's hand.

"Let me just grab you a saddle and—"

"I can do it."

Matthews bit his lip as Toni pushed past him to the array of saddles lined up in the corner. The saddle she chose was slightly different from what they had on the Purple Heart Ranch, but the mechanics were the same.

Matthews brought out another horse and had him saddled up while Toni was still fussing with the straps. A few seconds later, it looked like her time was up with the saddle. He took the straps from her hands and made quick work of the saddle. With that in place, he turned, his hands reaching for her. A zing went up and down Toni's spine as Matthews put a hand on either side of her waist. With a gasp, she smacked his hands from her body.

"What do you think you're doing?" she demanded.

"I'm helping you on the horse."

"I can get up myself."

"That's enough, Airman."

The rigidity and command in his voice made her snap to attention. Matthews always had a jovial look on his face. Even when things were serious. His expression was all flat lines as he regarded her now.

"You need help." His tone brooked no argument. "Whether you want to admit it or not, you need a helping hand. I have help to offer you. We're on the same mission."

"Fine."

"Fine."

They both stood with their arms crossed over their chest. Matthews moved first. He unfolded his arms and placed his hands on her waist again.

As she went up, Toni unfolded her arms. Her hands came to rest on his shoulders. She felt the play of muscles there as he lifted her up. Her breath caught as she looked down at him. She saw his pupils dilate and his nostrils flare. Was that heat she saw in his eyes? She'd never know because once she was settled down on the back of the horse, he turned from her.

Sitting astride the horse, Toni realized she didn't care. She'd lost so much of her power since that crash. She'd nearly lost her faculties when Matthews had lifted her off the ground. Now that she was on the horse, she felt she had her power back.

CHAPTER TEN

*T*opher knew this trail like the back of his hand.

He frowned at that saying as the words rolled through his head. He had never spent much time looking at the back of his hand. He doubted he'd be able to pick it out of a lineup of photographs. But if he saw the roots poking out of the ground on this trail, if he saw the wind of the path and the types of rocks that were off to the sides, if he saw the way the wildflowers grew, he would know he was on his favorite path.

He'd been walking it, running on it, riding on it for more than half his life. But he'd never brought a girl on it. Not even Tricksy during their ill-fated relationship—if you could call a few group dates to the ice cream shop and a couple of unfinessed kisses a relationship.

Tricksy had called that a relationship. Up until a couple weeks ago, she had called him the love of her life. In the same breath, she'd also called him her worst mistake.

That debacle, like his biological mother's heartbreak and his adoptive mom's death, taught Topher that love was not in his cards. Mostly because it was a game he had no interest in playing. Which was why he preferred to get in, have a little fun, then get out before feelings could develop.

Luckily, he didn't have to worry about feelings with Solis. He didn't think the woman had any. Not with how she grimaced and bared the physical pain she was clearly in. He saw that, like he'd had to scoop her injured body up and into his arms to save her life after the crash, he'd have to drag her bodily to get her to ask for the help it was clear she needed but for some reason was too stubborn to ask for.

He glanced over his shoulder at Solis. She wasn't even looking at him. She rarely did. Which meant he didn't have to worry about the idea of a relationship between the two of them entering her head.

All she wanted was to get well so that she could

return to the service. It was what he wanted too. Not just for himself, but for her, too.

Solis eyed the trail with a small smile. He'd never seen the woman smile before. It made her look like… well, like a woman. Almost pretty.

The two thick braids that wound around the crown of her head were crooked. They were always crooked, if he remembered correctly. She was often wearing a helmet, so he hadn't paid much attention.

The haphazard part down the middle of her head, which was out of alignment, made her appear more accessible. Like she was someone who could make a mistake and not worry too much about it. Much like the trail that stretched out before them, twisting and winding on a circuitous path. Topher wondered about running his fingers across that track in her hair.

He gave himself a shake. What was a thought like that doing in his head? This was Solis. She wasn't a woman. She was an airman. And he wouldn't be staying long enough to run his fingers anywhere on her body. His only interest in her body was getting it back in shape so she could move on with her life.

Her gaze caught his, and she frowned. That was another thing about her. Whenever women caught Topher looking, they never frowned. They smiled demurely, doing that hair flick thing or leaning forward with their chest on display—all those things to keep men's gazes lingering and offering an invitation. Solis's glare was a loud and clear door slammed shut.

"Your form is good," he said, trying to cover from his wayward eyes. "On the horse, I mean. I mean—riding the horse."

Topher pursed his lips. He'd never been tongue-tied around a woman before. Why was this one making him nervous?

"Thank you," she said, her shoulders straightening at the compliment.

Something sparked in Topher's chest. He liked what that compliment elicited from her. He wanted to see it again.

"You could loosen up on the reins a bit."

Her shoulders went rigid, but not like before. There was a stiffness to them now. The smile had dissolved from her face.

"I know the procedure to ride a horse. I aced the checklist they had at the Purple Heart Ranch."

"Is everything a checklist to you?"

"I like to be prepared. We can't all fly by the seat of our pants."

"I don't use my pants to fly."

"That's not what I heard."

She said it under her breath, but Topher heard it clearly. She likely meant it as an insult, but the joke was funny, and he laughed. She glared at him. Instead of a chin lift or a light in her eyes, she bristled. Of course she did. She was Solis.

"Who exactly did you hear it from?" he asked, curious to know which woman had kissed and told about him to her. He'd always thought her clipboard and pens were her only friends. He never saw her gossiping with the other female soldiers.

"Like you'd even remember their names," she said.

Wow, she was tough as nails. But she had the right of it. Topher didn't mind having a love-them-and-leave-them reputation. It made things easier when it was time for him to go.

"I'm surprised your family even remembers my name," she went on.

"I've never brought a woman home."

"Of course you haven't. No commitment on your part. Though Tricksy seems to have stuck around."

"Me and Tricks…" Topher sighed. "We're complicated. She followed me home because her sister Savy was dating my brother Charlie."

"And you plucked her off."

"There was no plucking. It was never real. Just—what do they call it? Puppy love."

"I wouldn't know. I'm a cat person."

Again, he laughed at the insult that he chose to interpret as a joke. Turning to face her, he caught her crack a smile. But it was there and gone so fast. Topher wracked his brain to determine how to get it back, how to make it linger. What came out of his mouth was a truth he rarely spoke of.

"I'm not the bad guy here. I don't believe in love. Not love like that. Not love between two people that are essentially strangers. Now the love between a parent and a child, that's different."

"You loved your biological parents?"

"No, they were both selfish people." Thinking about it now, Topher realized he might have a bit of their selfishness in him with how he interacted with the fairer sex. "My adoptive parents, they chose me. Even when I didn't deserve it, they still chose me. I can't imagine doing that with some random woman."

They rode in silence for a few yards. Topher wanted to fill the silence, but with what? He didn't know. He felt raw after having exposed that piece of himself. Would she turn around and use it to hurt him? She was a trained soldier.

"I'm no expert," Solis finally said at another turn in the path, "but I believe that's what dating is for."

Another non-joke. But this time, he didn't laugh. "That's not what dating is for."

"Pig."

Topher made a snorting sound that mimicked the animal he was accused of imitating. Solis laughed at him. A genuine laugh that time.

It had been a long time since he'd enjoyed his time with a woman without fear of her falling into imaginary love with him. Solis had zero interest in him. She'd made that clear. It allowed him to let his guard down even more.

"You don't have to worry about me falling for you," she said. "Again."

"Again?"

"I fell out of a plane because of you."

"I caught you."

There was a charged moment. He watched her throat work as she swallowed. Her eyes were huge in that round face of hers. Her chin tilted up so that all he saw was the crown of her braids and not the crooked part.

His smile was nervous, not the confident one he always wore around women, around anyone. He wanted to open his mouth to make an excuse, to joke the sentiment of those words away. But the words were out there. He couldn't take them back. And so he looked away.

"Any way," he went on, "I'm going to help you get back on your feet. I owe it to you."

"You don't owe me anything, Matthews. But... thank you."

He hadn't expected to hear those words. "You're welcome. Don't worry, you won't have to deal with me for long. I'll be deploying again soon."

The silence was deafening. He looked over, and the look on Solis's face was thunderous. Without any warning, she took off at a gallop.

CHAPTER ELEVEN

*T*oni leaned into the horse as it took off. The wind whipping against her face stung, but the air dried any tears before they could form. The bouncing of the horse made her leg throb as she fought to keep her seat, but better endure that pain in her knee than the ache scratching at her chest. She should stop before she fell, but it was already too late. And so she held on tight and urged the horse faster.

How had she fallen for it?

She was such a fool.

Her backside protested the rough ride. But Toni wasn't sure if it was that pain or the pain of the fall that had her running faster, farther.

She ducked her head to avoid a tree branch. She

heard her name being called in the distance. Matthews was chasing after her. But why?

Toni urged the horse faster. She'd never gone this fast before. The trainers at the Purple Heart Ranch had only ever let her go as fast as a trot. This was a full-on gallop, and she was close to losing control. But the power she felt, the freedom she felt atop the horse at this speed was too good to pull on the reins.

As long as she was moving forward, no one would leave her behind. As long as she was running, she wouldn't hear anyone's words to stop her in her tracks. Or worse, their silence wouldn't make her shiver with its cold completeness.

Except it wasn't silent out here on the trail.

Toni heard the sound of hooves pounding the ground behind her. She knew there were wild horses roaming free in this part of Montana. Was one joining her run?

A quick glance over her shoulders disabused her of that notion. It was Matthews. And he was gaining.

But why was he following her? He'd just said he was leaving. Leaving here. Leaving her.

Before those words had left his lips, Toni had felt high on the horse. She'd let that man lift her up on this pedestal, the pedestal of a horse at that. She'd learned he'd never brought a girl home. It felt like he'd never shared this special place with another woman, either. For a moment, Toni had felt special.

His talk of not believing in love didn't bother her. She didn't believe in it either. Her own father had made the choice to neglect her each day of her life since her mother's death. So no, she didn't expect Matthews's love. But she had warmed to the notion of being special to him.

Until he told her he'd be leaving her behind. Going back to work. Just like her father did every day of her life. Because she was a burden.

The tears stung her eyes now. The drops were falling too fast for the wind to catch them. She couldn't lift a hand to swipe them away. She couldn't let Matthews catch her. She couldn't let him see her like this. She couldn't.

"Toni!"

Matthews had never called her by her first name. She was surprised he even knew it. Her grip slipped on the reins, and she wobbled in the saddle.

Looking ahead, Toni saw a small log lying on the path. The mare would have to jump to clear it. Toni hadn't practiced jumping back at the Purple Heart Ranch. She had no clue of what to do. She was going to lose her seat and be thrown from the horse.

Gripping the reins, Toni pulled on them, trying to

slow the horse down. But she couldn't sit up straight to tug hard enough. It felt as if when she tried to right her body, she would lose her grip and fall.

"Toni!"

She dared a glance to her left and saw Matthews riding right beside her. He reached out his hand to her. But Toni was too frightened to grab for it.

"Give me your hand, soldier."

The command in his voice was absolute. She had to follow the order. But her fingers wouldn't loosen their death grip on the reins.

Cold seeped into her body under the warm glow of the midday sun. Her fingers were icicles as they curled around the leather. Her lips trembled and her teeth chattered as she ducked her head against the wind slamming into her face.

And then there was heat.

Matthews's warm hand was on hers. The reins were being taken from her. Mercifully, the horse began to slow until she came to a dead stop.

Toni could feel the animal's pounding heart against her thighs. It made her knee throb. Her hunched position made her shoulder ache.

And then she was weightless.

An arm came around her waist. She was

airborne, being lifted off the horse. She didn't fight it. But she did try to hide her face.

She was deposited with a deep, male grunt against a warm chest. An arm like a tight band came around her. The world slowed, but she felt another pounding all around her.

It was her heart. It pounded in her ear. Against her cheek.

No, that wasn't just her heart. It was Matthews's heart, too. He held on to her, breathing hard, squeezing tight.

It had been a long time since Toni had been held. She couldn't remember the last time. But she was sure it had been inside her mother's arms.

Her mother's arms had been strong. Her heartbeat a song Toni would remember always. Inside that embrace, Toni had felt safe, like she wasn't alone in the world.

She closed her eyes inside the safety of this hold. Her lips parted as she took in long, deep breaths that made her heart settle. The weight left her shoulders. The ache left her leg.

It was good. So good. Too good.

And then it was over.

Topher yanked her from him, far enough so that

he could peer down at her with a stormy glare in his eyes.

"What were you thinking? Were you even thinking?"

Toni opened her mouth. All that came out was a choked cry. Followed by a deluge of tears.

CHAPTER TWELVE

opher slammed the hammer against the nail. It sank in in just two whacks. That was a bit disappointing. He wanted to pound something harder and for much longer. He grabbed another nail and repeated the process.

This time, it took him four whacks. On the first try, his fingers shook, and he dropped the nail. On the second try, he just barely missed his thumb, and the nail went in crooked.

This had been happening for two days now. For two days, a tremble would turn up in his hands. For two days, his hands would ball into fists out of nowhere.

No, not out of nowhere. Anytime he caught a glimpse of Toni Solis peeking out of the window of the guest house. Anytime he caught sight of Mahalia grazing in her pen.

Topher didn't blame the old girl for what had happened out on the trail. He blamed Solis. He just didn't know why she'd done it.

She'd clammed up after he'd pulled her from the runaway horse and held her tight. At first, he hadn't been able to speak, hadn't been able to get a single word past the pounding of his heart. When her tears fell, he hadn't wanted to say anything else.

Topher was a trained soldier. He'd been battle tested first by the crazed warriors that had grown up with him on the ranch and then by the best military personnel on the face of the earth. But his Achilles' heel? A woman's tears.

He'd never expected a display like that from the stoic Solis. And he wanted to know why she'd done it. Why had she taken off like that? Was it something he'd said? He couldn't imagine what. And she wouldn't tell him. She wouldn't even talk to him.

When he'd knocked on the guest house door the day after, she hadn't answered. Not being one to push, he'd left her alone to lick her wounds and got to work.

The work to be done on the roof was grueling for one man. Joe was in the city every day, trying to save the world through the muddy water of local politics. Will had his hands full with the five foster kids that were learning the ropes on the ranch. And the roof was just the beginning of the repairs that needed to be done. Not to mention the ongoing upkeep of running the ranch.

The Silver sisters from the neighboring ranch had been by to lend a hand when they could. Those six women knew their way around the land since they'd grown up thinking of the Flying Cross ranch as an extended backyard. They'd been the ones helping out Father Matthews while his sons were away flying around the world.

But Topher couldn't expect the Silver girls to stop their lives to keep tending to the Matthewses' lands. Especially with their husbands glaring at him as their pregnant wives picked up construction tools and corralled wily animals.

Topher needed more hands on the ranch. There were another two pairs of hands that could be helping at the moment. So he picked up the phone and dialed.

While the phone rang, Topher looked toward the guest house. He could see shadows moving behind the curtain of the front window. No doubt Solis was inside working on her PT. He knew the woman had a list and was sticking to it religiously. He had a sudden ache to bust down the door and snatch the clipboard from her, just to have her glare at him with those hazel eyes.

"Brooooo." The truncated word was drawled out in a deep, masculine voice that sounded as though it hadn't been used yet this morning.

"Bro," Topher answered.

"You know what time it is here?"

Maybe it was still night where Mateo and Aldo were. There was a lilting quality to the words, letting Topher know he was talking to Aldo. Mateo had worked hard to eliminate as much of his Spanish accent as possible, where Aldo had embraced his Mexican heritage full bore.

Topher ignored Aldo's question. "We need you home."

There was a rustling of sheets. "Is it Dad?"

"Yes."

Topher heard his brother swear. Then he heard an identical voice swear. There were muffled sounds, and then a new voice came on the phone.

"Is it another heart attack?" asked Mateo.

"What? No. Dad's fine. He needs our help on the ranch. Things are in disrepair here. Charlie's on his honeymoon. Joe is slammed with his state foster care case. And Will is always making stupid eyes at Tricksy. Pretty sure he'll be wanting to go on a honeymoon soon."

"Is this about Tricksy?" Aldo drawled. "I thought you were over her."

"I was never under her."

There were boyish chuckles on the other end of the line. In their laughter, no one could tell the twins apart. Though Topher would always be able to guess who told the joke. Aldo was the trickster of their bunch.

"You two grow up," said Topher. "I'm being serious here. Dad needs help here."

"We'll be home soon. Meanwhile, he has you. Didn't you always say you could do the work of three men?"

"I can. But this isn't my only job right now."

The door to the guest house opened, and Solis came out. She tilted her head to the sun and pushed her hips forward, which also pushed her chest forward. Topher was far enough away that he couldn't see anything fun, but just the sight of her curves as she stood their unaware made his heart skip a beat.

He gave himself a shake. He should not be looking at that woman like that. He shouldn't even be looking at her like she was a woman. She was Solis.

"We heard about your little project from Charlie," said Mateo.

Topher pinched the bridge between his brows. "Does that man not know what to do on a honeymoon?"

"Sounds like you might be thinking of one yourself," said Aldo, his voice filled with mirth.

"What? No! It's not like that. I'm just helping her out until she gets back on her feet."

"By bringing her home and tending her wounds personally?" Aldo snickered.

"I owe her. It's my fault."

"You know better than to play that game, bro." Mateo's voice turned serious, leaving no room for joking. "We all know what we sign up for in this life."

All Topher could think about was watching Solis fall. Seeing the fear in her eyes. Then reaching for her, just like he'd done when she was on that galloping horse.

She'd closed her eyes then as Mahalia ran off with her. Closed them and seemed to accept her fate.

Well, screw that. Screw it then and screw it now. He wouldn't let her give up back on the battlefield. He wasn't letting her give up now.

He'd give her the rest of the day to sulk and lick her wounds, and then he was going to get back to tending to them himself. He'd have that soldier in ship shape before he deployed, and then they could all get back to the life they'd signed up for.

CHAPTER THIRTEEN

Toni stayed in bed as the sun rose. She didn't rise from the bed until the star was at its pinnacle in the sky. She puttered around the guest house all day, making sure to stay out of the sun's rays, sticking instead to the shadows, lest she be spotted. Now that the sun was starting to set and darkness was slowly creeping in, she finally poked her head outside the door.

The activity on the ranch had died down. There had only been one knock on her door. Foxy had stopped by to check on her and bring her a plate of food and herbal tea. A wary Tricksy had stood sentry in the background, her wavy hair pulled taut in a high ponytail that made her look like a disapproving warden and not a welcoming matron.

"I felt that you were hungry," Foxy had said.

"Felt?" Toni asked, taking the plate of food. As a kid who'd grown up on microwaveable foods and graduated to the mess hall of various army bases, she wasn't picky.

"I'm clairsentient," Foxy clarified.

Toni didn't point out that it was late in the day and it was a good bet that she would be hungry since she hadn't shown up for any of the appointed mealtimes. The guest house had a small fridge and a two-burner stove. But she was grateful for the home-cooked meal.

"And don't worry about Butch, the bus driver," Foxy continued. "His honk is worse than his bite."

With a smile and a wave, the woman bounced down the steps. Toni frowned at Foxy's retreating form.

Tricksy wrinkled her nose at her sister as she passed by. When Tricksy lifted her head, her and Toni's gazes connected. It would have been a shared moment, except Tricksy schooled her features and turned on her heel, effectively shutting Toni out.

Toni was used to that from other women. She hadn't had many girlfriends growing up. She hadn't had that many boyfriends either. And definitely not a real boyfriend. The school counselor had diagnosed Toni with attachment issues. That was before she left for a better job a couple of weeks later in private care. Though the counselor was gone, the diagnosis lingered. Toni didn't see the point in attaching to anyone when nobody was permanent in her life.

That's how she found herself later in the evening —sitting alone on the guest house porch without anyone else coming to check on her. She'd made it clear she didn't want or need company, and it looked like the Matthewses would respect that. Topher Matthews was clearly all too happy to keep his distance after she'd shed her tears, and that suited her just fine.

She reached for the end of one of her braids and began to uncoil it. Taking a fat-toothed comb, she ran the teeth through her hair, starting at the end. Toni had learned the hard way that any hair maintenance had to start at the end unless she wanted the mother of all headaches. That was a lesson she'd had to learn since she didn't have a mother to tend her hair, and her father didn't always remember to make her an appointment at the hair salon.

Toni's arms quickly began to tire as she went through the task of unraveling the second braid and pulling the comb through her tight curls. That ride had taxed her muscles, much more than it ever had on the Purple Heart Ranch. She'd never ridden that fast before. She had almost died before.

Twice now.

Twice she'd been trapped in a conveyance that she'd had no control over.

Twice she'd almost lost her life.

Twice Topher Matthews had been there to rescue her.

That craziness ended now. She didn't need rescuing. She was the rescuer.

It was time to get her rehabilitation back on track. She had her first doctor's visit at the VA clinic in just two days. She wouldn't ask any of the Matthewses for help getting there. She could Uber.

Though she barely had any cell phone service out here on the ranch. And when she tapped the ride share app, it was still searching for a driver twenty minutes later.

With three bars of service, she was able to pull up the local transit authority website. She saw the bus schedules listed. But she'd have to walk a mile up the road to catch the first of three buses that would take her to the clinic.

There; problem solved. A mile would tax her, but it would be worth it not to have to sit next to

Matthews, who clearly didn't want to be around her. Or sit sandwiched between a chatty Foxy, who spouted nonsense and a scowling Tricksy, who clearly still had a thing for Matthews.

Toni put her phone to the side. Her arms had had a good rest from being raised over her head to fuss with her hair. Now that all of her tresses were unwoven and combed through, it was time to part the sections and rebraid. This was her least favorite part of hair care.

"That's not straight."

Toni looked up to find LaTisha staring at her from the porch.

"Here, let me." The little girl stomped up the steps in red cowboy boots and held out her hand for the comb.

Toni hesitated. This was a child. Could she even part straight? But she couldn't do worse than her own weary hands. Toni handed over the comb.

She felt the little girl's hands in her hair. Then the blunt tooth of the comb as it tracked across her scalp. It brought to mind sitting on the ground between her mother's legs as she did her hair as a girl.

The sound of her mother's laughter rang loud and clear in Toni's ears. Her temple warmed where she remembered her mother pressing a kiss there. Toni gave a shake and let the memory fall away.

"Are you going to marry Mr. Topher?"

That made Toni shake anew. "No. We're not even dating. I don't date."

"You're a career woman? Like Ms. Tricksy? She's a singer. She's really good, too. When she's not singing about Mr. Topher. She's marrying Mr. Will, you know. Are you going to marry one of the other brothers?"

"I'm not marrying anybody."

"Oh."

Toni wasn't sure if that *oh* was condemnation, accusation, or repudiation. But that single word made her shrink into herself.

"I want to get married," LaTisha continued as she worked the comb to the middle of Toni's scalp. "And be a mom, and have a husband that's also a dad. Sometimes dads aren't husbands, and husbands aren't dads. I think it would be best if I married a boy who wanted to be both."

"That's smart."

"Yeah, I know. I'm at the top of my class."

Toni couldn't hide her smile at that. "You don't want a career?"

LaTisha made a tsking sound with her teeth.

"Being a mom is a career. It's Ms. Savy and Ms. Foxy's job to take care of us kids. But I don't want to foster. I want my own kids. Not all fosters are good kids. Ms. Savy says that's not always their fault. But I think sometimes it is. You can choose to behave."

LaTisha handed the comb to Toni. Before Toni could raise her hands to gather hair to start braiding, LaTisha's small fingers were weaving at the front of her head.

Toni sat back. Her shoulder blades rested against LaTisha's small body. She found that she was enjoying the feel of someone's hands in her hair so much that she didn't stop the little girl. If it looked bad, she'd just redo it later.

"Do you have a mom and dad?" LaTisha asked.

"Everyone has a mom and dad."

"Nope. Everyone has parents. Not all parents are moms and dads."

Wow, this kid was wise beyond her years. Toni didn't want to answer her. She felt that if she spoke about her mom while in this vulnerable position of having her hair braided, the tears from yesterday would return. But the words escaped her lips none the less.

"My mom died when I was a little girl."

"Was she a good mom?" asked LaTisha.

Toni nodded.

"Mine wasn't. She wasn't a mom. She was just my parent. But now I have two moms, so it worked out for me."

Toni looked up to see Foxy. She gave a wave. Toni waved back, as though to say it was okay for LaTisha to be here. Foxy gave her a smile and turned back to the house.

"Mr. Topher's a good guy," LaTisha said as she switched to start the other braid. "He plays games with us, even the girls. I think he'll be more than a parent. I think he'll make a good dad."

Toni would have disagreed. Matthews was leaving. She knew from experience that a good dad didn't leave their kids to their own defenses all the time.

CHAPTER FOURTEEN

Topher slammed the truck's gate closed after making sure the supplies were secure. Packed in the back was lumber for fencing, shingles for roofing, and some specialized feed for a few of the chickens who were looking a little too lean.

He'd run out of space after tossing in the feed, but he still had more supplies to get to. He'd just have to take another trip. Or ask Joe to grab it on his way home from the law offices he shared with Charlotte O'Dell.

The problem with that idea was that Joe drove a luxury car. His brother might not get upset if the interior got a little dirty. There was still enough farm boy in him. But that high end car wouldn't fit a quarter of the supplies Topher still needed brought back to the ranch.

He'd just have to make another trip. He couldn't do it later today, and he couldn't come back tomorrow. Tomorrow he had Solis's appointment at the VA clinic.

A small voice in his head whispered that he could have one of the girls drive Solis instead. Topher flapped his hand at his ear, like he would an annoying gnat. Solis was as much his responsibility as was the upkeep of the ranch. He could manage both while he was here.

There was still so much work to do on the ranch. Repairs that had been part of his and his brothers' chores growing up had been neglected. How had his father maintained all this time? How had they not noticed the ranch slowly falling into disrepair?

The same way they hadn't noticed their father getting older.

Haran Matthews had always been a giant to him. Topher still looked up to the man like he held the world on his shoulders. He just hadn't realized his father's shoulders were slumping from the weight he carried. For as long as he was here, he'd lessen that weight while not adding more onto his father's back.

Which meant he'd get Solis back on her feet. But

maybe not on a horse for a while. He could work out a loaner vehicle for her and show her around town and the way to the VA. Which meant he would have to finally go and see her at the guest house.

Climbing into the truck, Topher shoved the key into the ignition. The engine sputtered before turning over. Just another thing to add to his long list of chores. The twins had better get here soon to lift their own weight on the ranch, because Topher was starting to feel the ache in his own back.

Rounding Main Street, the engine sputtered again when Topher's foot slammed on the brake. Sitting at the bus stop was a sight he hadn't expected to see: Toni Solis.

She was hunched over, rubbing at her knee. It was her left knee, the injured one. He knew that because his arms had been covered in her blood when he'd scooped her up after the crash.

She pumped the leg in and out. A wince stayed on her face as she made the movements. Clearly, she was in pain.

Had she walked here? No, that wasn't possible. It was five miles from the ranch into town. But it was one mile from the ranch to the nearest bus stop. And there she sat, where the bus would have dropped her off.

Switching his foot from the brake to the gas, Topher pulled up to her at the bus stop. He slammed the truck into park and stared at her out the window. She looked up and started when she saw him.

"What are you doing?" he shouted.

"What does it look like?" she answered in that haughty tone of hers.

There was a sheen of sweat on her forehead. A trickle ran down her temple, making the tight curls at her nape cling to her neck. Topher felt an irrational sense of jealousy staring at those curls.

He lifted his gaze slightly to the crown of her head. Her hair was freshly braided. The rows in nice straight lines. The woven poufs made it look like an actual crown was sitting atop her head. Her nose in the air completed the regal look.

"How'd you get here?" he demanded.

Solis pursed her lips like an indignant child.

"Did Foxy or Tricksy give you a ride?"

She looked down the street at the bus ambling toward them. That answered the question for him. She had taken the bus. Which meant she'd walked to the stop.

Why? Why would she put herself, her body, through such an arduous task? Why hadn't she asked him for help? He would've taken her wherever she wanted to go.

"Where are you going?" The moment the words were out of his mouth, he held his breath, uncertain whether or not he wanted the answer.

"I'm doing a practice run for my appointment at the VA," she said. "I wanted to do the route before I had to actually go."

Topher's mouth gaped, but nothing came out for a full thirty seconds. Another second longer and he would've caught a fly. He chucked his thumb at his chest. "I'm taking you to the appointment."

"This time," she agreed with a nod. "But what about next week or next month? I need to make sure I can do it myself."

"When I'm gone, someone from my family will help you."

"I can't rely on your family."

"Of course you can." His family members were the most reliable people in the world. It's why he'd brought her here to them. He was getting nowhere with this conversation. Topher slammed the driver's side door open and hopped out.

"You can't park there. It's the bus lane. You'll get a fine."

"I'm responsible for you," he said.

"No you're not. You feel guilty. That'll wear off, and then I'll be right here, on my own."

"It's not guilt," he said, stepping up to her.

"Then what?" she came to standing, but she wobbled.

It was instinct. He reached for her. First to steady her. But once she was steady, he didn't let her go.

"I need to know you're safe," he said.

Solis's throat worked, but she couldn't get any words out. Good. He didn't want to hear any more lip from her.

Thinking about her lips, Topher couldn't help but dip his gaze to them. There were plump and lush. The type of lips that begged to be gently kissed and then bitten.

"We survived something traumatic," he said quietly. "That might not make us family, but it connects us."

She stared up at him with big eyes. He saw it again, the vulnerability he'd seen when he'd reached for her in the crash. The same look when he'd pulled her to him when the horse had taken off.

Couldn't she see that it was safe here? Safe with him.

"I need to know you're safe," he repeated. "Flying Cross is the safest place I know. My family will keep you safe if I'm not here. I want you to stay here, with them."

"For how long?"

He almost said forever. The word fluttered around inside his chest, banging at his lungs to get out. Instead, he said, "Stay until you feel independent enough to go."

He gazed down at her. The vulnerability was still there. Perhaps if he pulled her closer, it would—

HONK! The bus had pulled in behind his truck. In the driver's seat was Butch, the bus driver. The man had been running these routes since Topher was a kid. He loved to honk that horn, but he was unlikely to get out of the seat and do anything about it.

Topher corralled Solis to the passenger side of the truck while Butch leaned on his horn. Topher waited until Solis was safely inside and securely held by her seatbelt. Then he rounded to the driver's side. He caught sight of Butcher's glare in the rearview mirror as the man finally let up off the horn.

oni watched the flames as they rose into the night air. The sparks hissed as they twirled up into the dark sky, circling each other and fizzling out. It was as though the flames in the hearth couldn't contain themselves. They crackled and popped, sounding for all the world like the smack of kisses.

Not that Toni knew what kisses sounded like firsthand. She'd never been kissed herself. She had never been much interested in the act. At first glance, love looked like a warm and cozy thing, but she'd seen far too much heartache. The angry and despondent tears had always looked to her like they burned the rejected.

And so she kept her distance from the bonfire

and stood on the outskirts of the gathering. The people partaking of the fire's warmth were all couples. They stood with hands entwined, heads close together, bodies angled toward one another.

They were all from the neighboring Silver Star Ranch. A gaggle of six sisters and their husbands. Over a dozen people had introduced themselves to her. Toni was surprised she could remember all of the women's names. But then again, each Silver sister had a name related to the military.

The eldest, Scout, with her severe expression that softened each time her husband nuzzled into her neck. Sailor with a high ponytail and round belly who danced in her husband's one-armed embrace, even though there was no music playing. The prim and proper Mareen looked slightly out of place with her designer jeans and boots as she leaned against a green-eyed giant that reminded Toni of the Incredible Hulk. The giant's hands were gentle as they rested on the small bump at his wife's belly. There was even youthful Brigadere on the arm of a man who looked twice her age, but Brig carried herself in a way that seemed older than her years. And finally, the twins, Artillery and Gunnery, talked over one another and completed the other's sentences as their husbands watched them in mute fascination.

Each woman looked at Toni with friendly curiosity when Matthews led her to the spot. Someone had tossed a log into the pit, and the flames had sparked. Matthews had turned and angled his body so that she was shielded from the worst of the heat. Once the flames had settled, those friendly gazes had turned into open inquiry.

Toni had been peppered with questions about how long she'd known Matthews and how well. It had felt like an interrogation, done with pretty smiles and assessing gazes. The Silver sisters were the daughters of a general, but not a single one of them had joined the service. If they had, they would have managed world peace in under a week through sheer force of will.

Though she had no secrets to spill, Toni felt that she was close to cracking within the first five minutes. She managed to slip away when the two James sisters arrived, diverting attention away from her. Before she made her escape, her gaze locked with Matthews's.

It had been doing that since they'd arrived at the impromptu bonfire. It had been doing that on the drive back from town. It had been doing that over the dinner table as the foster children had all talked over one another, laughing and poking fun at one another while the adults refereed or joined in the ribbing.

Matthews's gazes were quick assessments. Rhetorical questions he clearly wasn't expecting verbal answers to. His blue eyes seemed to ask her the same thing each time.

Are you okay?

He never gave her leave to answer. His gaze would simply meet hers. Then he would do a quick scan of her person. Toni wasn't sure what his metric was to gauge her well-being, but she appeared to pass each time.

It was only his gaze that he rested upon her, and briefly. He didn't come within arm's reach of her again. He didn't reach for her again. He didn't glance at her mouth as though her lips were twin flames that he wanted to warm himself near.

In fact, a few times when she got close to him, his body jerked back from her. As though she might burn him. Clearly, he was regretting whatever it was that had passed between them earlier. If it had been anything at all.

Which it hadn't. He just felt responsible for her. He might deny his guilty feelings about the crash, but she knew that was all this was. He would be gone soon, and soon after his departure, she planned to make hers.

She was no one's charity case. She could take care of herself. She'd never liked being coddled.

Well, she hadn't thought she'd like it. She'd never actually been coddled. Though it was nice having his gaze search her out every now and again.

She felt his eyes on her as she stole between the trees. The hiss and crackle of the fire mingled with the babbling of the brook just beyond the bonfire. Her body was tired from the long walk she'd taken this morning, but she wasn't limping. The land was flat, with no stairs to climb or logs to step over. Picking up a stone, Toni rubbed the smooth surface and then let it rip.

Plop plop plop plop—splash!

Not so bad. She was almost back to her stone-skipping record. Looking down at the ground, she searched for another stone that would help prove that she was on the mend and returning to her former glory. She spied two candidates and bent down to retrieve them.

"He watches you."

Still in her crouch, Toni glanced over her shoulder to find Tricksy watching her. Toni didn't need to ask who *he* was. She also didn't feel like she owed this woman a response, especially not after the six-way Silver interrogation she'd just made it through. But she technically was a guest here where Tricksy lived.

"Matthews feels responsible for what happened to me," Toni offered up. "That's all."

"So you're saying it's guilt he's feeling and not love?" Tricksy's hands were clasped behind her back as she took slow steps toward Toni, looking for all the world like a lawyer who was making the case against a clearly guilty defendant. "Because trust me, that man doesn't believe in love."

Neither did Toni, but she didn't tell this woman that. However, there was something else she wanted to know. "Why do you care? I thought you were with his brother."

Tricksy unclasped her hands from behind her back and brought them up to her heart. "I am. I'm with Will."

Toni came to standing, the rocks in the palm of her hand. Not as weapons to use against the other woman. Even though Tricksy clearly regarded her as a foe.

"I love him," Tricksy was saying. "Will, I mean. I really love him. Not like some little girl crush or puppy love. The real thing, you know?"

Toni did not know. So she said nothing.

"Topher isn't capable of the real thing. So I'm just warning you; don't fall for him."

"Are you sure you haven't gotten up from that fall you had for him?"

Tricksy's pretty features soured. The light in her eyes when she had been talking about Will died a quick death as she glared at Toni. The rocks in her palm made a clicking sound as Toni rubbed them together.

"Look," Toni said, "I'm just here to get better and then I'm out. Topher's headed back into the service, anyway. There's nothing between us but duty."

Tricksy made a noncommittal sound. Toni thought the woman would argue more. Instead, she turned on her heel. But she didn't get far.

Standing in the path was Matthews. Like he had been doing all day, his gaze found Toni and did its assessment. Once he appeared to satisfy himself that Toni was in good health, he turned an ice blue glare on Tricksy.

CHAPTER SIXTEEN

The bonfire took place at a spot halfway between the Flying Cross Ranch and the Silver Star Ranch. It was neutral territory, so to speak. A place that both families claimed as their own. Though truly the only reason for fencing between the two ranches was for the animals and not the wild children who roamed free.

Topher knew both ranches like the back of his hand, which he had been studying of late. He knew how many paces it would take to go from the bonfire pit to the little creek. He knew what trees sprang from each side of the path and where their roots unfurled from the ground. He knew the path was well trodden with little to no tripping hazards.

He knew the water was shallow, with no danger of drowning.

All these things he knew so well, but he itched to follow Solis to the clearing. The hairs at the nape of his neck prickled with the need to ensure that she was safe and well. There was a tickle at the corner of his eye where he needed to see for himself that she hadn't tripped over a new vine that may have sprung up since his last visit to this well-known spot.

His feet were moving before he finished making any demand of his body. But his progress was slowed as he fielded questions from the Silver sisters. Scout made kissing noises behind his back, something he would've had a witty comeback for just a couple of days ago, but now he let the childish action go as he picked up his steps.

Solis had been withdrawn for most of the party. He'd thought she might be fatigued if not over-whelmed by the nagging nosiness of those silver hellcats. He was sure the only reason their husbands put up with the girls was due to their time in boot camp.

Breaking free of the landmines his neighbors tried and failed to toss his way, Topher hurried down the path. Then slowed his steps. He didn't want to appear overeager. He was simply doing his duty, handling his responsibility.

The irritation that was scratching at his chest at having Solis out of his sight for more than a minute was due to his concern for her and her well-being. Nothing more.

She'd looked weary as she'd progressively made her way to the edges of the gathering. He'd been about to suggest she call it a night when she'd walked off. When he saw the direction of her steps, he relaxed a bit. He knew she liked water, had an affinity for it. He'd caught her on base skipping stones a few times. He'd watched silently, smug in the knowledge that he could best her in number of skips.

She was likely headed there to skip stones. Now would be a great time to challenge her. And just to make sure she was doing okay. Because she was his responsibility. And because of the panic he'd felt seeing her sitting at that bus stop this morning.

It had been the same panic he'd felt when he'd caught her gaze as he'd lost control of the aircraft. It had been the same panic he'd felt when she'd gone galloping ahead of him.

Topher knew the woman always had a plan. But he liked it best when he was the one in the cockpit when her plans were set in motion. He wanted to be the one in the driver's seat as her strategies were played out. He wanted to be in the lead when the orderly procedures she'd prescribed were initiated.

When he came into the clearing, he saw that someone else had beaten him to the helm. Tricksy paced before Solis, throwing kinks into an operation that had nothing to do with her.

"I thought we got past this, Tricks," Topher said.

Tricksy stiffened and looked up at him. For a moment, she looked like a kid caught with her hand in the cookie jar. He'd seen that look on her face before. He'd been the one next to her when she'd tried to steal the cookies, after all. She'd gotten in trouble, but he'd escaped.

Another woman who had gotten a scrape in her dealings with him. But Tricksy was all right now. She was head over heels in love with his brother, who should've been her first love in the first place. Not Topher.

"Oh, I am so over you, Christopher Matthews." Tricksy spat his full name like it was a bad taste in her mouth. "I've found real love with Will."

"Yeah, I know." Topher shrugged. "And I'm happy for you. I'm happy for you both. So what gives?" Topher made a motion between her and Solis, who stood at attention with her hands behind her back, like the good soldier she was.

"I'm just trying to mitigate any damage you might do to anyone else." Tricksy jutted her chin up at him.

That chin was as sharp as a sword, but the blow she'd tried to deal him was dull. He knew he'd hurt his old friend. Tricksy was the first, and the last woman whom he'd both befriended and dated. After the nightmare that was their breakup, Topher had sworn never to go down that road again.

Over the years, he'd missed Tricksy's friendship. He hadn't heard her laugh or seen her smile in years. Whenever she looked at him, it was with pain or anger in her eyes.

Topher's gaze found Solis. She didn't pretend to not listen. Her right palm was in motion, making clicking noises as she rubbed two stones together. She was trying to smooth the rough edges of the rocks before she flung them into the water. Unlike the stones in her hands, Topher's rough edges would never be smoothed away.

"You break every girl's heart you come in contact with," Tricksy was saying.

"We're not dating," both Topher and Solis said at the same time.

"Oh, please," said Tricksy. "I've seen the way you look at him."

Had she looked at him in some way? He only ever saw judgment and disappointment in Solis's gaze when he saw his reflection there. In answer, there was a crunching sound as Solis ground the rocks in her hands. Her eyes went wide, and her nose wrinkled.

"And I've seen the way you look at her." Tricksy pointed an accusing finger at Topher.

Now Topher's features reformed to incredulity. The only reason he looked at Solis was to assess her health and well-being. Sure, he'd started noticing other things about her. Like how her body curved in all the right ways outside of fatigues. With her hair parted straight, he noticed how it crowned her head. With her head up and not looking down at documents, he saw how her lips were heart-shaped and not a thin, judgmental line.

"You leave hurt behind," said Tricksy. "And the thing is, I don't think you mean to do it. You just can't help yourself."

And with that last missive hurled his way, Tricksy stormed back up the path. Topher stood stunned into stillness in the wake of her destruction.

No, he didn't mean to do it. But how was it his

fault that women expected more from him than he was willing to give? He never lied. And when he was bluntly honest, it always made things even worse.

"Do you need to be alone?" asked Solis.

Her voice was a siren in the darkness. Topher stepped closer to it.

"There's no such thing as alone here," he said. The silence stretched between them, and he knew she would've let it linger. But he felt the need to fill it. "She's wrong."

"You do have the hots for me?"

The comment was so unexpected, it caught him entirely off guard. With his center of gravity knocked off its axis, he threw back his head and laughed. When the world felt steady again, he turned to look at her. In the moonlight, she looked more than pretty. Before she could catch him staring, Topher bent to pick up a few stones.

CHAPTER SEVENTEEN

*H*is hands were large. His fingers slim and agile. They didn't look soft or gentle. They did look capable, and they proved that they were as the stone skimmed across the surface of the water five times before making a splash and sinking into the dark waters.

Toni lifted an eyebrow. He had impressive skill. She would've said so, but she was enjoying the silence between them. Plus, if she kept quiet, she didn't have to admit that she thought he was good. The man's head was already big enough.

Except that it wasn't. His head was perfectly normal-sized, capped with those blond tufts of hair that moved with him as he put his whole body into his tosses.

Those blue eyes shone with a light that said he knew how good he was. He knew how attractive he was. He knew that she thought so. He inclined his head as though to tell her to simply give up trying to hide her attraction to him and admit it.

"Do you give up?" he asked.

"What?"

"It's your turn." He made a motion with those slim, agile fingers.

Toni swallowed. Her heart made a series of fast thumps inside her chest like it was skipping across the water. When she tore her gaze from his hand to look up into those blue eyes, she heard a decided thud and was surprised to see that she was still standing.

Matthews was talking about the game they had slipped into. He was talking about her turn at tossing a rock. Nothing else.

Intellectually, she knew that. Logically, she knew that. Sensibly, she knew that. There was no reason for her heart to have all these theatrics. No reason for her head to see something that wasn't there.

With a deep breath, Toni stepped up to the water's edge. She rubbed the two rocks she held in her palm against one another. The grating sound like nails on a chalkboard calmed her senses, or at least distracted them enough away from the silly thoughts she'd been engaging in a moment ago.

With a flick of her wrist, she sent one stone flying. *Plop plop plop plop...plop—splash!*

"Yes!" she shouted, throwing fists in the air. It was five plops, just one shy of her highest score of six. But she hadn't managed this many in months. Just more proof that she was truly on the mend, almost back to her old self.

Next to her, Matthews let out a low laugh. It was the second time he'd laughed at her antics this night. The first being after the joke she'd made about him having the hots for her.

It had been an absurd thing to say, but she'd hated the silence left behind when Tricksy had stormed off. Though Toni had the distinct feeling that Matthews hadn't been laughing at her when he'd thrown back his head and chuckled. He wasn't laughing at her now, either. He seemed relaxed and delighted... by her.

As the last of his laughter subsided, a grin remained on his face. He gazed down at her, his features further softening. Those blue eyes of his were hooded, but she saw something in them. She just wasn't sure what.

Interest?

Curiosity?

Toni knew she should move away from him. She had heard what Tricksy had said about him breaking hearts. She'd seen it with her own eyes back on the base. But she had never thought for a second that he was interested in her. He had never even looked at her. Not really.

He was looking at her now, his gaze taking in her features. What was he seeing?

Was it because she was the only woman out here to seduce? He usually was grinning or smirking at women when he was seducing them. She'd seen it because she'd watched him.

Toni's breath caught when his fingertips made impact on her temple. She'd been right about his fingers not being gentle. There were calluses on the pads of his thumb and index finger. Still, it was the softest touch she'd ever experienced.

It was the only tender touch she'd ever experienced like this, besides her fading memories of her mother. Definitely, no man had ever touched her like this.

She knew she should turn away. She knew she should pull back. Topher Matthews was a heartbreaker, and she was a wounded warrior.

Toni tilted her head back to receive the kiss he

was about to steal from her. Because she was a trained soldier, and she would prefer to be at the ready to meet this mission. His lips did not crash down on hers. Instead, his fingers tangled in her hair.

"You've come undone," he said.

Toni blinked.

"Your hair. It's come undone."

Reaching up, Toni felt the free strands of her hair had come loose from its braid. She jerked away from Matthews. Giving him her back, she tried to work her fingers through the strands.

"I'm sorry," he said. "I know better than to touch a woman's hair without permission. I was just... I mean..."

He hadn't been trying to steal a kiss. He hadn't been preparing for a carnal attack. She wasn't beautiful to him. She wasn't desirable. She probably looked like a wild thing with her hair out.

"You're not parting it straight," he said. "Here, let me help."

He reached for her again. But she didn't want him to see her like this. However, the moment his fingers slid into her hair, it short-circuited her resolve.

Matthews's fingers weren't only in her hair, they

were moving about the strands. Toni felt the edge of his nail as he parted the hair down to her scalp.

She thought that was it. But he didn't stop at the part. He towered over her, moving to her side and tilting her head for easier access. And then he began to weave her hair back into submission.

For long moments, Toni stood silent. Partly in shock that a young, White man was braiding a Black woman's hair. Mostly in a stunned sort of paralysis at how good his movements around the crown of her head felt.

"How do you know how to braid hair?" she asked.

"My mom. My adoptive mom. I saw her doing it to her hair one day, and I was curious. So she taught me."

His adoptive father was African American. There was a good chance Father Matthews' wife had been Black as well. Toni was certain the woman was Black when she reached up and felt the secure braid on the side of her head.

"There," he said. "Beautiful."

"You think I'm beautiful?" As soon as the words were out of her mouth, she wanted to take them back.

Matthews shrugged. "Of course you are. You're

one of the few women who is and doesn't act like she knows it. I've always liked that about you."

Well, the joke was on him because she didn't know she was beautiful. She was fairly certain that she wasn't. But she wasn't going to argue with him. She wasn't even sure what to say now that he'd put her back together atop her head while everything inside was in an upwhirl.

"I'm not going to hurt you, Toni."

Right. Because he wasn't interested in dating her. So why did she have a sudden tinge of pain?

CHAPTER EIGHTEEN

opher pulled the truck door open for Toni as she came down the steps. Her gait was fine this morning, the limp not as pronounced. Her braids were straight, which made his nose wrinkle a bit. He liked it when she was a bit crooked. He wondered if that was still the same braid he'd woven into her hair last night out by the water.

His fingers clenched to a fist to try to dispel the itch that descended on the palm of his hand. He'd enjoyed the feel of her thick hair in his hands as he'd weaved the strands together. Solis had always appeared formidable to him, but her hair had followed his every command without a strand coming loose in protest.

Topher wished she'd come undone again. He wished he'd left behind a straggler that would give him the excuse to undo the braid, all so he could weave the loose strand back in line. But she was completely put together today.

She glanced up at him then. A shy expression shone in those coffee-colored eyes. Then she glanced away.

He resisted the urge to hand her into the truck. Well, he tried to. Without conscious thought, his hand raised to assist her. And wonder of wonders, she took it. The moment her fingertips met his palm, there was a zing of electricity between them.

He heard her gasp. His fingers closed around hers before she could pull away. But the spark was there and gone by then. And she was seated in the passenger seat. Leaving him no reason to hold on to her.

Topher shut Toni inside. The click of the latch was loud in his ears. He about faced and began to walk around the truck to the driver's side. Instead of heading around the front end of the car, he decided to take the long way around the back. His steps slowed as he got to the driver's side as realization dawned.

Solis was going to be fine. She was going to

completely recover from her injuries. And then she was going to leave. The meeting at the VA clinic would likely confirm it today.

How long would they give her? Likely another month? Maybe two? Definitely not longer than the six months he would be deployed. She'd be gone before he got back.

Then she'd likely be on a mission of her own. There was no guarantee they'd serve together again. No guarantee they'd have more time together in the future.

Topher scratched at his heart. With his other hand, he leaned against the driver's side door before opening it. He ran his hand over the back of his head, tugging at the overlong locks of his hair.

This was a good thing. This was the goal they'd both hoped to achieve. She was getting better, and he would be leaving. His debt to her would be repaid.

This was a good thing. These were all good things. Yet the itch at his chest persisted.

Across the way, Topher caught a glimpse of Tricksy. She was giving him that evil eye that she'd given to him ever since they were kids and she claimed he'd broken her heart. The itch at his chest ceased, and he gave his former friend his back.

Climbing in the truck, Topher put the vehicle in gear and pulled away from the ranch, leaving Tricksy in the rearview mirror.

The drive to the hospital was a quiet one. He appreciated that about Solis. She didn't care for idle chitchat. It was always about the mission for her.

On the radio, Mahalia Jackson crooned as they drove. Solis held a clipboard in her hand. On it, he saw a number of check marks next to her neat script. But he couldn't make out the script and keep his eyes on the road at the same time. Besides, he didn't need to know what gains Solis had made in her healing to return to active duty. He knew the woman was going to ace any exam the doctors gave her.

Taking one hand off the wheel, Topher scratched again at the itch at his chest. Foxy must have replaced the detergent in the laundry room with some environmental brand that he was having an allergic reaction to.

He parked in the visitor's lot as close to the entrance as he could get. Solis reached for the passenger side door handle. Topher's gaze landed on her hand. She must have felt the heat of his glare, because when their gazes connected, she put her hand back in her lap and looked forward. Topher couldn't hide the smile that lit his lips as he got out of the truck and went around to her side.

He offered his hand after opening the door. She took it, just lightly resting her fingertips on his palm. Topher's fingers curled around hers reflexively. She didn't pull away. Instead, she stepped down gingerly.

He glanced at a wheelchair and raised a brow. She snatched her hand from his and punched him in the shoulder with it. He was still laughing as they made their way into the clinic.

He was also still rubbing at his shoulder. Despite the woman being small and carrying around a shoulder injury, she had a good right hook. She was going to be fine.

Topher stood by quietly as she filled out the paperwork. His gaze rested on the braid in her hair. Even though she could throw a punch, she still struggled with her hair. If they were stationed together again, would she let him part it for her? Would she let him braid it?

A single strand had come loose from the end of the braid. It curled around the base of her neck. He should tell her. Or maybe he should fix it for her.

"You don't have to stay," she said.

Topher crossed his arms over his chest. He pressed his fists into his sides under his armpits as he did so. A glance in a mirror might have him resembling a toddler on the verge of a tantrum.

He wasn't going anywhere until he knew the timeline of when she was leaving. Finally, they were called back. Topher rose to go with her, but the nurse raised his hand.

"Sorry," said the male nurse in a shirt with colorful umbrellas. "Family only."

Solis's face went blank. Her coffee-colored gaze turned to a bitter shade as she looked everywhere but at Topher.

"I am her family," said Topher.

"Oh, my mistake." The nurse grinned. "Fiancés are welcome."

Topher saw Solis swallow hard, but she said nothing. So neither did he, and the nurse lead them both back.

The doctor was a middle-aged male that looked like he had once been a drill sergeant. His biceps were fairly bursting out of his white coat. His shoulders were back, his feet braced apart as he got down to the questions.

"Any new injuries?" he asked.

"No," answered Toni.

"Yes," said Topher.

They both turned to him.

"She was nearly thrown from a horse. Before that, she was riding pretty hard. I haven't seen her in any pain, but she often hides it well."

The doctor nodded, jotting down some notes.

Toni's mouth hung open as she looked at him incredulously.

Topher wasn't sorry for it. He wanted the doctor to have all the facts to make the best decision possible about Solis's future.

"Any prescriptions or non-prescription medications?"

"No," said Toni.

"My sister-in-law has been giving her echinacea tea and willow bark tinctures the last two days."

"Matthews!"

Topher shrugged, keeping his attention on the doctor and his note-taking. The man didn't bother to hide his grin, likely thinking they were, in fact, a soon to be married couple squabbling. At another time, Topher would've shuddered at the notion. Instead, he crossed his arms tighter over his chest and waited for the next question.

"I'm sure a cup of tea doesn't matter," Solis was saying.

"It's good to inform your healthcare provider about herbal remedies," said the doctor as he continued to scribble notes. "Their healing effects are widely known in the scientific community and have been known to impact some medications."

"I just want to know what I need to do to get back out there."

The doctor lifted his head then. "Back out there?"

"Back to active duty. Just give me the list of things I need to do and..." Toni's voice trailed off as she saw the doctor's expression.

"I'm sorry, Airman Solis. Your injuries are career ending. There is no going back on active duty."

CHAPTER NINETEEN

Everything hurt. The passenger seat had suddenly sprung coils that dug into Toni's back and sides. There was no longer enough leg room, and her knees ached from being in a tight crouch. The leather of the seat was hot to the touch. The windowpane was freezing cold. She needed to get out of here.

"Pull over."

"We'll be home in a minute," said Matthews, moving one hand over the other as he made a turn onto the Main Street of the small town.

Home? Toni didn't have a home. The one place she had felt like she had belonged had just denied her from ever returning.

She couldn't go back. They didn't want her back. So where was she going to go?

Her breaths came quick and shallow. Though she panted while turned toward the window, there was no chance for the air from her lungs to fog up the glass. No sooner did one puff present itself than the next breath of air wiped the vapors away.

"I need to get out," she said.

Matthews sent her a glance. His blue eyes shone clear in the passenger side window. She'd seen that worried look only one time before: the time just before he'd lost control of the aircraft and they'd crashed.

He hadn't been in control of that situation. Neither had she. She hadn't planned for that disaster, and she had no plan for the new blow dealt her. The military no longer wanted her.

Toni was this close to yanking open the door and leaping out when Matthews slowed and came to a stop. Toni looked up to note it was at the same bus stop from the other day. Luckily for him, the bus was nowhere in sight.

What did this mean that he'd brought her here? Did he want her to get on the bus now? Was her time up with him and his family now that there was no hope for her reinstatement?

"Are you going to be sick?" Matthews's hands reached for her but came short of touching her.

Toni's hand went to the door handle. She didn't wait for him to come around and hand her out like some dainty lady. She wasn't a dainty lady. She was a soldier.

No matter whether they wanted her or not. She was a soldier.

She yanked open the door and spilled out. Her foot hit the ground wrong, causing her knees to buckle. She bent over, but she didn't collapse onto the ground.

Strong arms came around her, lifting her back up. Toni was pulled into a warm chest. Arms came around to hold her steady. Hands pressed the back of her head against a thudding heartbeat.

Toni wanted to push against him. She wanted to fight him. But it felt too good. It felt too necessary when her world was falling apart around her.

And so she let Matthews hold her.

From the corner of her eye, she saw people glancing at them. She didn't care. Her lifelong dream had just been snatched away from her. When Matthews let her go, she would be facing a world of darkness.

"I'm going to have to go home," she said. Toni felt his nod as his cheek moved along her temple.

"I'll take you home."

"Not your home," she said, shaking her head against his chest. But she only managed two shakes before resting her head back at the center of his chest where his heartbeat was the strongest. "Not back to the ranch. I have to go to my father's home."

Matthews's hold tightened on her. His heartbeat kicked up a notch. He blew out a breath that sailed down the center of her head where he'd parted her hair into a straight line the other night.

"That is, if he's even there," Toni went on in the silence. "He's very dedicated to his career and often spends nights at his office."

Matthews said nothing. He only held on to her. When Toni shifted to break his hold, she felt the reluctance with which he let her go.

"Stay," he finally managed to say, though the word sounded choked. Like it had been forced out of him.

"I can't impose on your family indefinitely."

"You are my—" he cleared his throat. "I want you to stay."

"Why?"

"It's my fault."

Toni didn't need him to clarify what he was at fault for. "It's not your fault, and you know it. We all knew what we signed up for."

"I should've gone over your mission readiness list one more time. I should've..." Matthews sighed, resting his forehead against hers.

They were still standing apart. He didn't put his arms around her again. He just stood there, resting his blond locks against her dark braids.

Even though he wasn't touching her, Toni could taste his breath. She could feel his heat. He opened his eyes and stared into hers. His gaze landed on her mouth.

Toni's lips parted of their own accord. The tip of her tongue dipped out to moisten first her lower and then her top lip. But he didn't come any closer.

Matthews straightened but didn't back away from her. He blinked a couple of times, as though he was waking from a dream.

"I'm going to be leaving," he said. "I'll be deployed for six months."

The disappointment was bitter at the back of Toni's throat. Could this day get any worse? She'd lost her career. Had no place to go. And she'd made a fool of herself in front of the one man she wanted to see her as strong and brave.

"Maybe I'll just go back to the Purple Heart Ranch and marry some random soldier so I can live there."

Matthews's blue eyes iced over. His hands curled into fists.

When he'd been mistaken for her fiancé back at the hospital, he hadn't said anything. Neither had she. Toni had secretly liked the feel of having that title placed on him. She had liked the notion of having someone that was hers.

Topher Matthews was so strong. So confident. So cocky. He was the type of man that would save a damsel in distress. He'd saved her more than once. He hadn't left her behind. Not on the battlefield. Not in her rehabilitation. She could stay with him. She could—

"Topher Matthews, is that you?"

Matthews glanced to the side without turning his head. His brows went down in concentration, as though he was trying to place the owner of the voice who'd called out to him.

"Up to your old tricks, seducing some poor woman on the street?"

Toni saw his dilemma in placing the voice. It wasn't just one voice. It was a group of girls. Or rather women, if their shapely figures in sundresses and heeled sandals were anything to go by. In turn, each one of them lifted a brow as they looked at Toni. Those brows lowered almost instantly in what looked like dismissal.

"Everyone's taken a ride on that train," said one. "Enjoy it while it lasts, sweetie."

She hadn't even had the chance to get on the ride. Because she wasn't the type of girl who he rode around with. She wasn't the type of woman men stayed around for.

CHAPTER TWENTY

Topher watched the guest house until the light went off. The drive home had been a tense and silent one. He wasn't sure what he'd done wrong, but he knew it was something.

It was probably that almost kiss. Whenever he kissed a woman, it was inevitably the beginning of the end of their time together. He wasn't ready for his time with Toni Solis to be over. Which is why he'd pulled away from her before he could mess things up.

Unfortunately, it hadn't worked. He'd still messed things up without even tasting those lush lips that had tilted up to meet his. He should've at least done the crime now that he was forced to serve this silent time out.

The silence he could handle. But only if it was temporary. He did not want her to go. At least not without fixing whatever he'd done wrong.

No, that wasn't right. Even after he fixed it, he still wanted her here. Still wanted her to stay on the ranch. He couldn't stand the idea of her going to an empty home with an absentee father. She needed someone to care for her.

It wouldn't be him. He would be gone soon. But his family would care for her. His father would take her in as one of his own. His brothers would ensure no harm came to her. His sisters-in-law would keep her company. He...?

He could what?

He didn't know what?

He just knew he didn't want her to be out in the world and he not know where she was, how she was doing. What if she tried to walk too far and re-injured herself? What if she tried to ride another horse and pushed herself so hard she was thrown? What if she went back for another doctor's visit and she neglected to tell him all the medicinals she was taking and something went wrong?

No. He couldn't let her go. She had to stay here where there would be people to look after her.

People he trusted to keep her healing and happy. Until he could return to her. And… what?

He still didn't know the answer to that when the guest house light went out. Topher had been half paralyzed with fear that she'd sneak away in the middle of the night and he would never see her again. Never hold her. Never touch her.

He'd almost kissed her. If he'd kissed her, he knew he'd never see her again. That's how it went with him. He never stayed with a woman. His lovers always wound up getting their hearts broken, even though he never meant to handle that organ.

Dating was meant to be fun. He didn't know why women took it so seriously. Why they expected forever. He wasn't the forever guy. Not unless they were family.

He wanted Toni to be a part of this family and stay forever. If he'd kissed her, like he wanted to do, then she would have her heart broken. And he didn't want either of those things to happen.

A creak on the floorboard put him on alert. Topher knew it wasn't one of his brothers. They'd learned the art of stealth when they were boys. No, that creak was deliberate. The person wanted to be heard.

"Hey, Tricks."

"What'd you do to her?"

The hair at the nape of his neck stiffened. "I didn't do anything."

Tricksy stood with her arms crossed over her chest looking for all the world like the young girl he used to be friends with. His gaze went unfocused as he tried to reconcile the two. The bright-eyed girl with a big voice along with this creature who always wore a sour expression as she shouted into a microphone about being done wrong.

Despite it all, Topher missed being friends with her. He missed her playfulness and laughter. He even missed the sound of her singing voice. He just didn't want to hear another note from that song about their breakup. Though maybe he should listen to the anthem before he saw Solis again. To remind him how, after he'd kissed his friend, things had changed, and they'd never been the same again.

"She can't go back into the military," Topher admitted.

"I'm sorry to hear that."

"She's going to leave."

"Why?" Tricksy's gaze narrowed, and her lips curled. "What did you do?"

Topher sighed. The evening breeze brought a

dull awareness to his body. This was a pointless conversation.

"She's in love with you."

He doubted that. But he couldn't be sure. It wasn't something he looked for in the women he dated. It wasn't something he was interested in knowing.

"Do you care about her at all?"

"Of course, I do. I want to help her get better, to help her keep healing. I want her to stay here and be with people who care about her. I don't want her to go out into the world alone where I can't be sure she'll be looked after."

He hadn't realized he'd started pacing the length of the porch until the sound of his boots stomping out a staccato rhythm broke his attention. He looked again to the darkened guest house.

"She's so strong, but she's vulnerable. She has a talent for thinking of every possibility, of every eventuality in a battle, but she still has blind spots. What if she misses a blind spot and I—" He cleared his throat and began again. "What if she doesn't have someone there to watch her back?"

Tricksy was silent as she regarded him. Topher held still under her scrutiny. He could only stand it for so long before he took up his pacing again.

"Why am I even telling you this? I'm the villain in your story. I'll always be the villain. And that's fine."

He reached the end of the porch and was confronted again with the darkened guest house. He wanted to go over there, to knock on the door and… And what?

Instead, he rounded on Tricksy. "You know what, no it's not. You continuing to cast me as the villain is not fine. I cared about you back then. I've never stopped caring about you. But just because I didn't feel the same way as you did doesn't make me the bad guy forever."

Tricksy's arms remained crossed over her shoulders as she took slow, careful steps toward him. "No, it doesn't."

Topher braced himself for an attack. But no blow came. Still, he remained on his guard. Those James sisters had grown up alongside the Matthewses. They knew how to throw a punch, especially when a guy was down.

"I saw it," she said. "I saw it the moment she stepped onto this ranch."

"You saw what?"

"That she was different. That you were different with her. You don't look at her like you do other girls."

"How do I look at her?"

"Like you care."

"I cared about you, Tricks. I care about you."

"Yeah, like family."

Topher didn't see how that was a bad thing. She was family. But she also wasn't hitting him and was having a conversation with him at normal volume. So he stayed quiet and let her continue.

"I watched you look at other girls back then. You would look through them like they were all the same. You always looked at me and saw me, just not in the way I wanted you to see me."

Topher had no idea what she meant. He mostly tried to avoid her gazes when she came over for dinner, or there was a holiday gathering, or they were out at a town event with their families. But he couldn't entirely avoid watching out for her. Especially when he knew a few guys had been after her, thinking to take advantage of her broken heart. He'd used his fists to set them straight each time.

"Even though you stopped looking at me, I knew that you saw me," Tricksy was saying. "When you look at Toni, it's like you see into her. It's like she's all you see."

That's because Solis was easy to read. She was an

open book, if you knew how to read the signs. Or better yet, like reading a radar screen.

She was all blips and lines to others. But to his eyes, it was a perfect map. And he knew what her charted course would be.

"She's going to leave," he said.

"Tell her you want her to stay."

"I did. She thinks she's imposing. That woman is violently independent."

"Then use your charm on her."

"Then she would definitely leave. It always goes south after I date a woman. I don't want things to go south with her. I don't want her to go anywhere."

"Then use your charm on her."

"Then she would definitely leave. It always goes south after I date a woman. I don't want things to go south with her. I don't want her to go anywhere. I want her to stay here for as long as she wants."

Topher knew he was repeating himself. But he was very clear on what he wanted and what he didn't want. No other words were necessary.

"Wow." Tricksy rested a hand on his shoulder. "You've got it bad."

Topher didn't want to explain to Tricksy how he always lost interest in women after he'd kissed them. He didn't want to remind her that they always blew up at him when they realized their feelings for him were more than his feelings for them. He was sure that the reminder would unravel the fragile peace that had settled between them.

"Besides," he went on, "I have to leave soon."

"But you're coming back."

"I always come back."

"If you want her to be here when you do, then you'll need to give her a reason to stay. Or preferably more than one."

"Like a list? Like a checklist?"

"Sure, that—"

A blinding lightbulb went off in Topher's head. He bent down and smacked a kiss on Tricksy's cheek. "Thanks, Tricks. I think I know what to do."

Her gaze on him was one of pure bewilderment. She rubbed at the place where he'd kissed her and then looked quizzically at her fingertips.

"Tricks?"

"Yeah?"

"Are we really good this time?"

She punched him in the shoulder with the hand she'd used to wipe at the kiss. "We're getting there."

CHAPTER TWENTY-ONE

oni was up before the sun. She'd watched it go down last night. She'd kept the moon company while it did its nocturnal work. She'd been there to greet the sun after the moon went to bed.

She didn't have much time left. Her bags were packed and stacked by the door. She just needed to be sure of her direction.

Spying her phone sitting on the charger on the counter, Toni went to pick up the device to map out her new course. But when she reached for it, her hand skidded past the device and landed on a comb. It was the comb Latisha had used to part her hair a couple of days ago.

Toni's gaze went around the entire cabin. The

James girls had made it cozy for her stay, adding a few personal touches that were slightly masculine, but still worked for Toni. She'd felt cozy here. But this was not her place.

She couldn't stay when Topher left on deployment. She couldn't stay while he was still here visiting with his family. She didn't want to feel like an outsider. She'd felt like that her whole life.

Turning her back on the interior of the cabin, she sat down the comb and picked up her phone. Then she dialed the number she'd known by heart since she was a child before she could talk herself out of it. The phone rang and rang. And then rang some more.

Just as she thought it would go to voice mail a deep male voice answered.

"Antonia?"

"Hi, Dad."

"Is there a problem with your recovery?"

Her heart quickened. There was a fluttery sensation in her stomach. "No, Daddy. I'm all right. I'm fine. I—"

"Good," he sighed.

The weight of that sigh landed like a stone in her gut, stilling the flutters. Her heartbeat slowed so abruptly, she felt the thud in her heels which caused her to rock back.

"I'm preparing for a lecture," he went on. "Can we reschedule this call? I have some time on Tuesday between 3:30 and 4:45. Will that work for you?"

Toni heard the click of his pen open. She envisioned him drawing a neat little column on the scheduler on his clipboard to write her in. Likely in a small corner, with a perfect square to check her off his list when the appointed time came.

Toni opened her mouth to respond, but she choked on the words she wanted to say. Because she wasn't sure what to say?

"Antonia, I have to get back to my notes. Why don't you send me an email with the dates and times that work best for you and I'll do my best to fit you in? Have a good day."

Cell phones no longer clicked when disconnected. The line simply went dead. She was left on her own by the one person in the world that was supposed to care for her. Again.

She needed fresh air. But the last thing she wanted to do was bump into Matthews. Looking outside, she saw that no one was about at the front of the house, and so she stepped outside.

She also needed a ride into town. But she didn't

want to ask for help from anyone from this family. She didn't want them to know how alone she was. Not when there was so much togetherness here.

Maybe she could find Tricksy. That woman hated Matthews. Toni doubted Tricksy would be sad to see her go.

Out the window, she spotted her in the distance with those telltale dark curls. Tricksy was getting out of the car with two other men. One of them with skin a dark shade of brown like hers.

It was Matthews's father. He climbed out of the car and turned to her with a smile. That smile softened into a slight frown. His brows drew as he regarded her.

"Hey, Toni. Good morning," said the woman Toni had mistaken as Tricksy. It was her older sister Savy with her lush hair pulled back.

Savy looked bright and fresh and happy. Of course she did. She'd just come off her honeymoon.

"You coming in for breakfast? I can't wait to show everyone the pictures."

"I was just going for a walk," said Toni.

"Mind if I walk with you?" asked Father Matthews. "Been on a boat for days and then in that car for hours. I need to stretch my legs on solid earth."

Toni wasn't sure how to turn the man down. Standing under the soft glow of his kind smile, she wasn't sure she wanted to leave his warm light. And so she fell in step beside him.

The two walked in silence for a few moments. Toni kept a slow pace for him, but she somehow thought he was going slowly for her. Could he tell her injury was bothering her today?

"I'm sorry I haven't been here to help you," said Father Matthews. "I know that's what my son was hoping for. My boys seem to think I have a way of fixing their problems."

"I'm not your son's problem."

"No, my dear. You're not a problem at all. You're a solution for him, which is the problem." Father Matthews chuckled at his private joke.

"There's nothing between..."

Toni let the sentence die because it wasn't true. There was something between them. At least on her part. She might not have experience in relationships, but she knew a spark when she felt it. This spark was going to fizzle because it burned all by itself in a pit with no kindling.

"He was right to bring you here."

Toni shook her head. "I can't stay."

"I would be sad to see you go."

"You don't even know me."

"Exactly." His grin was wide. "I'd like a chance to get to know the woman who's stolen my son's heart."

"I don't have his heart. He hasn't even kissed me."

The moment the words were out, she blushed. Thankfully, her cheeks wouldn't turn a telltale shade of red, but she was certain Father Matthews could feel the heat coming off them.

"Topher was the kind of kid who destroyed toys. Race cars with only three wheels. Toy soldiers missing arms and legs. But there was one he kept in a box and never played with because it was the most special to him."

"You're saying I'm a toy in a box?"

Father Matthews canted his head. "You could stay and find out."

"You're inviting me to stay even though your son is leaving?"

"I'm inviting you to stay because it's clear you need help. It's even clearer you don't know how to ask for it. So I'll make it easy for you—"

He didn't have a chance to finish his sentence. Not when a sob escaped from Toni. Quickly, she pressed her hand to her mouth. But the sob would not be held back.

She'd held it down for so long, but her shoulders

were weary from the injury. The blow her own father had just dealt her had ripped at the bandages. Now she was standing before a stranger with her raw emotions exposed.

Father Matthews took hold of her shoulders. He turned her to face him, but she wouldn't raise her head. She didn't need to. He tucked her into his barrel chest and held her while the tears came.

He didn't make shushing noises. He didn't rub her back to hurry the tears out. He didn't tell her things would be okay with time. He didn't loosen his hold, signaling the end of his comfort. He simply stood there, lending his support for as long as she needed.

Toni didn't know how long they stood there like that. But slowly, her strength returned to her, and she felt strong enough to do what she knew needed to be done. She stepped out of Father Matthews's hold and put her shoulders straight. Her injury still ached, her heart was heavy with her own father's rejection, her spirit low from the knowledge that she wouldn't return to her career.

"I need help," she said.

Father Matthews held out his arm, like a gentleman caller would do. Toni took his arm as they walked back toward the guest house.

CHAPTER TWENTY-TWO

opher had seen her walk off with his father. He knew that was a good start. His father was good at making lost souls feel welcome. But Topher knew that he would have to be the one to convince Toni to stay.

He paced the length of the guest house porch, clipboard in hand. He patted the clipboard at his thigh; the nerves getting to him.

He always felt calm before a mission. He would rush into a sky full of danger and not break a sweat. Now his heart kept skipping beats. Sweat ran down his temple. His fingers cramped from the tight fists he kept clenching them into.

He couldn't fail at this task. It might be the most important of his life.

When he spied them in the distance, he knew the moment Toni caught sight of him. Her shoulders had been relaxed as she'd walked arm in arm with his father. There was a shy smile on her face as she nodded a bit, listened a lot, and spoke little.

Topher's dad had that effect on people. They instantly trusted him. Which was why he'd brought Toni home to him.

He'd wanted her trust. Somehow, he knew he couldn't gain it on his own. Not with his reputation. He needed to show her where he'd come from so that she might be willing to go with him where he wanted to journey next.

Topher hadn't truly understood the trajectory his life would take when he scooped Toni Solis into his arms that day after the crash. He'd just known that once he'd picked her up, he had not wanted to let her go.

Even now, he wanted to rush out to her. He wanted to peer down at the ground before she took any step to make sure no danger was set before her. He wanted to lift her and carry her in his arms so that nothing could touch her. He wanted to hold her close so that nothing could come between them.

He wanted to kiss her. Oh, how he wanted to kiss her. He cursed himself for not taking a shot at every chance that had come before when he'd turned away from her.

It hadn't been out of respect. It had been out of fear, fear of what she made him feel.

He had feelings for her. Were those feelings love? He supposed so.

The itching in his chest when he thought of her, the skipping of beats when she was near, the rapid-fire beats when she gave him a half smile, all those went beyond desire, beyond lust.

It was an ache that he felt. That ache was in every crevice of his body, and it never went away. Not when she was near. Not when she was away. Not when he was simply thinking of her. It was always there, had been since the day he'd first met her. He just hadn't understood it. He did now.

Those sensations, those feelings, were telling him to stay near this woman because she had found her way into his heart.

"Hey," she said, when she arrived at the steps to the porch.

"We need to talk."

Those were words Topher Matthews had always dreaded. Today, they were the beginning of the most important speech he'd make this far in his life. He'd made a plan of what to say. But his plan went out the window the moment she bit her lower lip.

He reached for her. The clipboard clattered to the ground as he brought her to him and crashed his mouth into hers.

She was at ease in his arms. He had her full attention. Her head tilted up to him in a salute and she presented her arms around his neck as he took another half step closer to her.

It was a kiss to end all kisses. It was a kiss that told him he ain't seen nothing yet. He didn't need to see anything more.

Toni's arms wove around his neck. Her fingers tangled in his hair. She made a soft mewling sound that ignited his hunger, and he pulled her even closer to deepen the kiss.

"Stay," he said.

"Okay," she whispered. Her eyes were dazed. Her lips parted as though she was expecting another assault and was ready for it.

"I was expecting a fight."

"It's the logical thing to do if I want to get better."

Logic. Right, she was a rational woman. And he must be losing his touch because that kiss should have made her completely irrational.

"And there's also the fact that I'm falling in love with you."

It wasn't the first time Topher had heard those words. In the past, it had always made him cut and run. He pulled Toni closer with one hand. With the other, he tugged one of her hands from around his neck and placed it over his heart.

"I'm pretty sure I'm falling in love with you, too." The smile that spread across her mouth had him hungering for another taste of her lips. "I've never felt this before. I'm not entirely sure what to do."

"We'll make a list."

"I already did." Topher bent and picked up the clipboard.

Toni grinned when she took it from him. Topher felt his heart skip a beat. That's when the last doubt of what he was feeling fled his mind. There was no falling involved. He was in the thick of it.

"Mission to be the Top Boyfriend."

Topher wanted to snatch the clipboard back so that he could scratch out that word boyfriend and replace it with something else. But all in due time.

"Does my plan meet your approval?" he asked.

"This is an excellent plan," she said.

"I remember you saying something about mindless repetition. We could practice item four, which covers dates and kisses."

She giggled at that, and Topher was certain it was the best sound he'd ever heard in his life.

"I figure we can go over it as much as we need before I deploy."

That word offered some levity to the situation.

"I'm coming back," he said.

"I don't doubt it," she said. "I'm gonna get better."

"I don't doubt it."

"Maybe not well enough for active duty, but I'm not finished with the military."

"We'll figure out our next steps together."

"That sounds like the perfect plan."

"I don't understand how we got stuck buying female supplies."

Mateo Matthews watched as his brother tossed a box of feminine products into the shopping cart. The cardboard box of supplies for a woman's time of the month landed with a dull splat at the bottom of the cart. Mateo lifted the box with a smiling woman on it who definitely did not look as though she were suffering from a feminine ailment and placed it back on the shelf. "That's not the right one."

"Oh, you're an expert in feminine hygiene now?" asked Aldo.

"No, I just know how to read instructions, and Savy specifically wrote down a different name brand."

Replacing the purple box, Mateo grabbed the pink brand of products from the shelf and placed them in the cart. With that last item on their shopping list checked off, they were down on the shopping excursion in town. They'd only been back home for a couple of days, and it was busier than usual on the ranch with all the Matthews boys home at once, a house full of foster kids, three James sisters, and Topher's new girlfriend who was living in the guest house.

With the rest of the adults having their hands full with ranch chores, repairs, and the general chaos that came with caring for foster kids, Mateo had offered to run errands in town for Savy. He hadn't expected his brother to come along on the domestic mission. But just like when they were kids, Aldo still suffered a bit from separation anxiety.

"The way you act sometimes, *hermano,* you'd think these were for you."

Mateo didn't think for a second that listening to the needs of another person meant that he was somehow feminine. In fact, he didn't think there was anything wrong with listening or with femininity.

"You need to knock it off," said Aldo. "It's ruining my rep."

"You do know that just because we're twins doesn't mean we share the same reputation."

Aldo scoffed at that.

Inwardly, Mateo scoffed, too.

For much of their lives, everyone around them linked the two with the other's behavior because of the way they looked. As identical twins, they looked exactly alike. Though their foster brothers and adoptive parents could always tell them apart. But to others, there was no distinction. So Mateo got blamed for a lot of the antics Aldo got up to, whether he agreed with what his brother got up to or not.

A lot of times, he did not agree.

Especially not the times when Aldo's mean streak made an appearance. Mateo was the lover where Aldo was the fighter. Not so much a fist fighter as a loud mouth.

Aldo had grown up a bully. Not because their biological parents had mistreated their kids. Their parents had wanted nothing but the best for their boys. They just hadn't been able to give it to them, and instead had lost everything when they'd tried.

The social workers and school counselors all said Aldo's bullying was all about self sabotaging. He didn't trust that he couldn't have anything good, so he tried to destroy any potential blessings before they could be taken away from him.

Mateo never had anything bad to say about anyone or anything. But because he looked like his brother, people didn't make the distinction between the two, especially not since Mateo often held his tongue and stood by when his brother went off at the mouth.

But for the first time in their lives, the Matthews twins' paths were about to diverge. Mateo was staying home after this last deployment, where Aldo was planned to go back into the service. While they were apart, Mateo hoped to settle down, build his own reputation apart from his twin, and perhaps even start to date. He wouldn't admit to his brother that he had one hometown girl in mind.

A certain red head with kind eyes and freckles dotting her cheeks. Green eyes like a dense forest that Mateo got lost in when he daydreamed. And smiling pink lips that made him think of the heart-shaped hard candies he'd once left at her desk on Valentine's Day.

"Hey look, it's Raggedy Ann."

Mateo frowned. He didn't see a red haired doll with yarn for hair and a button nose anywhere in the shop. Belatedly, he remembered that that was the mean nickname his brother had given to the exact girl Mateo had just been daydreaming of. Then, looking up, he caught sight of that beauty.

Kailyn Jade stood in the produce section of the grocery store. There was a shopping basket on one arm, and she held a carrot in her hand. Her gaze was wide, like a deer in headlights, as she stared up at Mateo.

Just like when he was young, Mateo ached to go up to her. To reach out and offer his hand in friendship. To tell her a funny joke, to see her grin go wide and those freckles spread. To give her a heart shaped candy that said *Be Mine* on it.

But just like when they were young, Kailyn's cheeks went red when she was in his presence, making those freckles disappear in the blush. Those green eyes that he wanted to keep focused on him dropped to the ground. And her slender shoulders hunched forward, like she'd been dealt a blow.

"And, look," Aldo continued. "There's Andy."

"Oh, would you look at that," said a carbon copy of Kailyn, but with bone straight red hair devoid of curls and a pair of glasses set low on her nose. "It's a walking, talking feminine product. Too bad it won't fit down the toilet for a flush. It needs to be taken out with the garbage."

The malicious grin dropped from Aldo's face and he looked ready for war. Facing off against him, Elayne Jade looked ready to deal the first strike in a battle that had been started years ago, but ended in a bitter stalemate.

Mateo opened his mouth, ready at last to defuse this decades long feud between the town's two sets of twins. But it was Kailyn's soft voice that broke through the tension.

"We have somewhere to be Elayne." Kailyn glanced at Mateo and his closed mouth before turning away from him with a dismissive shake of her head. "They're not worth it."

And with that, the Jade twins walked away from the Matthews twins. Mateo was left standing beside his brother, looking for the world like a solitary *they* when he just wanted to be a *me.* It looked like his dream of asking Kailyn Jade to be a we with him would never come true.

Mateo's got his work cut out for him.
You'll have to grab the next book to see if he can find
a way to sweep

Kailyn off her feet despite their two warring
siblings.

You don't want to miss the final two books and the
last two Matthews brothers.

The family saga continues with
Vow to Respect,
Book Five in the Flying Cross Ranch romances.

Shanae Johnson was raised by Saturday Morning cartoons and After School Specials. She still doesn't understand why there isn't a life lesson that ties the issues of the day together just before bedtime. While she's still waiting for the meaning of it all, she writes stories to try and figure it all out. Her books are wholesome and sweet, but her are heroes are hot and heroines are full of sass!

And by the way, the E elongates the A. So it's pronounced Shan-aaaaaaaa. Perfect for a hero to call out across the moors, or up to a balcony, or to blare outside her window on a boombox. If you hear him calling her name, please send him her way!

You can sign up for Shanae's Reader Group and receive a FREE NOVELLA in this world at

https://shanaejohnson.com/ReaderGroup

ALSO BY SHANAE JOHNSON

a Flying Cross Ranch Romance

His Vow to Love

His Vow to Treasure

His Vow to Adore

His Vow to Trust

His Vow to Respect

His Vow to Defend

The Silver Star Ranch Romances

His Pledge to Honor

His Pledge to Cherish

His Pledge to Protect

His Pledge to Obey

His Pledge to Have

His Pledge to Hold

The Brides of Purple Heart

On His Bended Knee

Hand Over His Heart

Offering His Arm

His Permanent Scar

Having His Back

In Over His Head

Always On His Mind

Every Step He Takes

In His Good Hands